Lasting
Impressions

By the same author

LASTING
IMPRESSIONS

Essays 1961–1987

V. S. PRITCHETT

Random House
New York

All rights reserved under International and Pan-American Copyright Conventions.
Published in the United States by Random House, Inc., New York.
The stories in this work were originally published in the *London Review of Books,*
New Statesman, The New Yorker, The New York Review of Books,
and *The New York Times.*

Library of Congress Cataloging-in-Publication Data

Pritchett, V. S. (Victor Sawdon), 1900–
[Essays. Selections]
Lasting impressions : essays 1961–1987 / by V. S. Pritchett.
p. cm.
ISBN 0-394-58720-0
I. Title
PR6031.R7A6 1990
809—dc20 90-8427

Manufactured in the United States of America
24689753
First Edition

For Dorothy

Contents

Sholom Aleichem   PAIN AND LAUGHTER 11

Isaac Babel   FIVE MINUTES OF LIFE 16

Simone de Beauvoir   GROWING OLD 20

Gerald Brenan   THE SAYINGS OF DON GERALDO 29

Robert Browning   PIONEER 35

Bruce Chatwin   WELSH PEASANTS 42

Flaubert & Turgenev   SPECTATORS 48

Humboldt   UNIVERSAL MAN 53

Molly Keane   IRISH BEHAVIOUR 58

Le Roy Ladurie   MEDIEVAL VOICES 64

Lorca   THE DEATH OF LORCA 72

André Malraux   MALRAUX AND PICASSO 77

Thomas Mann   THE ROMANTIC AGONY 83

V. S. Naipaul   IRAN AND PAKISTAN 90

George Orwell   THE CRYSTAL SPIRIT 96

John Osborne   A BETTER CLASS OF PERSON 100

Walker Percy   CLOWNS 107

Forrest Reid   ESCAPING FROM BELFAST 111

Salman Rushdie   MIDNIGHT'S CHILDREN 116

Antoine de Saint-Exupéry   LOST IN THE STARS 123

Bruno Schulz   COMIC GENIUS 128

Bernard Shaw   THE STAMP OF THE PURITAN 133

John Updike   GETTING RICHER 139

Rebecca West   ONE OF NATURE'S BALKANS 146

Oscar Wilde   AN ANGLO–IRISHMAN 151

P.G. Wodehouse   NEVER-NEVER-LAND 156

Mary Wollstonecraft   THE STRENGTH OF AN
   INJURED SPIRIT 163

LIST OF BOOKS 169

[7]

Preface

When I look back on my seventy years as a writer, I see myself as a traveller not only on the long journeys I have made in Europe and the Americas, but also as a literary journalist. Although I have written long biographical studies of Chekhov, Turgenev and Balzac, I have, as a short story writer, preferred the shorter evocations and I have profited by the discipline imposed by limited space.

This collection of literary essays – my ninth – may appear to be a haphazard journey through different countries and different generations, from Lorca to John Updike, from Browning to Wilde, but my purpose has always been the same: to *explore* the writers and their intentions.

I should like to thank the editors of the publications in which these pieces first appeared for helping me on my literary travels and for their permission to reprint them here.

Sholom Aleichem

PAIN AND LAUGHTER

———

Sholom Aleichem is one of the prolific masters of Yiddish comic storytelling, an art springing from the oral folk traditions of Eastern Europe and crossed by the pain and laughter of racial calamity. Like all comics he is serious, has one foot in the disorder and madness of the world and, as a Jew, the other foot in the now perplexing, now exalted, adjuration of the Law and the Prophets. Did God really choose their fate for the Jewish people? If so, was He being irresponsible, or why doesn't He make it clear? There is no answer. The oppressed stick to their rituals and are obliged to perfect the delights of cunning, the consolations of extravagant fantasy, the ironies and pedantries of the moralist who is privately turning his resignation into a weapon. With so many insoluble dilemmas on his hands, Aleichem developed that nimbleness of mind and fancy, those skills of masking and ventriloquism, that made him the prolific 'natural' in short tales drawn partly from the remaking of folk tradition, a juggler of puns, proverbs, and sudden revealing images caught from the bewildered tongues of his people.

There are certain distinctions to be noted when we speak of the general Jewish gift for anecdote. These are made clear in the exchange of letters between Irving Howe and Ruth Wisse which introduce their selection from a striking variety of Aleichem's best work and discuss the growth of mind it reveals. Mr Howe points out that Aleichem is not a 'folksy tickler of Jewish vanities' and the Yiddish folk material he uses is not as cosy 'as later generations of Jews have liked to suppose'. Under the laughter is fright and the old driving forces of anxiety and guilt: if Aleichem is close to folk sources he escapes the collective claustrophobia of a folk tradition that was broken by the pogroms and wars that drove the Eastern European Jews to flight or death; he has let in the light of 'a complicated and individual vision of human existence. That means terror and joy, dark and bright, fear and play.'

Ruth Wisse points to Aleichem's position in the period when the Jewish moral crisis came to a head in Eastern Europe. Writing of his contemporaries, the classical masters Mendele Mocher Sforim and I. L. Peretz, she says that they are embattled writers, 'fiercely critical of their society', strong in dialectical tendency, pitting old against new; whereas Aleichem, who also felt the break in the Jewish tradition and in his own life, 'makes it his artistic business to *close* the gap. In fact, wherever the danger of dissolution is greatest, the stories work their magic in simulating or creating a *terra firma*.' I do not know the work of these writers but it is certainly true of Aleichem's work that it shows his balance and poise in tales like 'A Yom Kippur Scandal', 'Station Baranovich', the terrifying 'Krushniker Delegation', 'Eternal Life', and above all in the four grave Tevye tales. As he tries to face his daughters' rebellion against tradition Tevye becomes, tragically, something more than a folk figure: he becomes a man.

Aleichem has the style of the spontaneous talker, at home in many garrulous idioms; it is a style that plays as it moves forward dramatically and then, hit by an image or a proverb, circles back. The narrator's mind is continually split between what is happening and something else, some fear, some scheme, some hope that is going on in his mind. He acts on impulse and regrets at once; always escaping from his situation, he is back in it only to find it changed, usually for the worse. He writes as a man backing away from the next minute and going headlong into it. Nearly all of Aleichem's people are whirled around by their imaginations, addressing fate, knocked this way and then that by scripture or the proverbs – 'When a soup bone is stuck in somebody's face who doesn't give it a lick?' On second thoughts, 'You can skin a bear in the forest but you still can't sell its hide there.' Speculation is their anguish. They burn with a fever. 'My blood began to whistle like a teakettle.' Aleichem's powers of invention pour out of the language he utters. The innumerable surprises of language so entangle us that we are caught out by the vaster surprises of the tale. In catching us out, his art shows its depth.

Aleichem's people themselves belong to a storytelling culture. He is as astonished and disturbed by his bizarre tales as we are and uses the device of not bringing them to an end, sometimes in order to show that the meaning of the tale has been hidden and we must work it out for ourselves or go on making it up on our own. This is evidence of a very self-conscious art, as Mr Howe says.

A clear example is 'A Yom Kippur Scandal'. A stranger comes to the synagogue and overcomes mistrust by handing out silver coins, but when the rituals are over, he suddenly screams out that he has been robbed of 1800 roubles, on the holiest day of the year. He had put the money into the praying stand and it has gone. The rabbi and his congregation turn out their pockets. Only one person refuses. He is a young man notorious for knowing the Talmud by heart, for being a master of Hebrew, arithmetic, algebra, unequalled in chess – perfection. The congregation argue with him, he begs to be spared, but they throw him to the ground and, going through his pockets discover only a couple of gnawed chicken bones and a dozen plum pits still wet from chewing.

> You can imagine what an impression this made – to discover food in the pockets of our prodigy on this holiest of fast days. Can you imagine the look on the young man's face, and on his father-in-law's? And on that of our poor rabbi?

But what about the 1800 roubles? Never found. Gone forever, says the storyteller, and never explains. We can suspect, if we like, that the stranger had invented the drama, to cover up the fact that he had stolen his employer's money. But Aleichem does not explain. Why not? Because the deeper sin than the sin of theft is the sin against God and His Law? Aleichem still doesn't say. We are perhaps left to search our own souls. Who knows?

'Station Baranovich' is another tale that stops short of its ending. It is told by a Jewish stranger on a train and is an event that occurred in czarist times. A loose-tongued bartender called Kivke starts a religious argument with peasants on a Sunday. He is reported to the police and is sentenced to be stripped naked and to run a gauntlet of cavalry officers, who will whip him. The Jews unite to plot his escape. They fake the death of Kivke in prison, arrange a mock funeral, and get him out of the country. He shows his gratitude by blackmailing them for larger and larger sums of money now that he is free. The final threat is to report the whole thing to the Russian Commissioner. But at this point the train stops at Baranovich and the teller of the story jumps out. What happened next, what is the end? the listeners shout. All they get is

'What end? It was just the beginning!'

and he is gone. Aleichem says

May Station Baranovich burn to the ground!

What does he mean? Ruth Wisse says it sounds like a protest against his own art or a defence of it. More likely it seems to me that the end being 'just the beginning' evokes the only too familiar frightful prospect that awaited the Jews of that village, a further test of their emotions, their ingenuity as an oppressed people.

Aleichem's humour has a double edge; it is concerned with a good deal of trickery or with efforts to bring off a successful or kind action which come to disaster because of some helpless absent-mindedness. In 'Eternal Life' the green young theological student who lives under the thumb of his mother-in-law volunteers, out of a desire to do a good deed that will win him Eternal Life, to take the body of a dead mother to the burial ground, because the father cannot leave the house and has no sleigh. The journey through the blizzard is terrible, so terrible that he cannot remember the name of the dead woman. So he is mad enough to make up the tale that the body is his mother-in-law's; she has died of fright. The inspector of the Burial Society asks, What sort of fright?

My tongue seemed to stick to my palate. I decided that, since I had begun with lies, I might as well continue with lies, and I made up a long tale about my mother-in-law sitting alone, knitting a sock, forgetting that her son Ephraim was there, a boy of thirteen, overgrown and a complete fool. He was playing with his shadow. He stole up to her, waved his hands over her head and uttered a goat cry, *Mehh!* He was making a shadow goat on the wall. And at this sound my mother-in-law fell from her stool and died.

[14]

Again and again, the storyteller invents other selves when he dramatises a dilemma. Yet this story is not mechanical farce; it passes through the moods of youthful exultation and sorrow, and as the blizzard drives him almost into sleep on the sleigh, the idea of Eternal Life has the sweetness of death and then turns to terror, for the wind seems to be the voice of the dead woman on the sleigh. She seems to accuse him and say, What are you doing to me, young man? Destroying a daughter of Israel who has died?

In this story we move through joy, exaltation, fear, and farce, as if these were a weather in which the people live. Indeed in all the stories, the feelings bound from one to another. The characters repeat themselves with comic fervour, as if searching for guarantees; they dramatise themselves as if they were momentary universes. Each in turn is the only one who loves, hates, scolds, whines, tricks or believes. In their voices these people, who have no land, have their territory and thus Aleichem has written its history.

Irving Howe notes that the Mottel farces introduce a Tom Sawyer-like note, which one does not hear in the adult stories. I notice something like a theme of Flann O'Brien's in one of them, My Brother Elye's Drink – in 'Mottel the Cantor's Son'. It is about a boy out to make a fortune from homemade kvass and ink, and who even offers to rid his town of mice. One can see Aleichem's instant, restless eye unfitted him for the novel. As the Tevye stories show, he could be grave without encumbering himself with novelistic architecture. One surprise is the almost complete lack of erotic or mystical fantasy, such as we find in I. B. Singer.

Isaac Babel

FIVE MINUTES OF LIFE

Isaac Babel was the most *telling* writer of abrupt stories to come out of the Russian revolution. This gentle Jew was a man who hit one in the belly. More important he had – what is indispensable to short stories – a distinct voice. Made famous by *Red Cavalry* and the Odessa stories – he was rewarded with a very pretty dacha – he worked under Gorki's influence and protection as a writer precariously accepted by the regime but increasingly restless and finally silent under it as a person and an artist; he was allowed to go to Paris and Italy, but his foreign contacts must have brought him under suspicion; he was arrested, secretly tried, and presumably executed, in the general Stalinist attack on the arts in 1939. A blunt story – rather like one of his own. His works vanished; references to them were cut out of histories and criticism; his manuscripts and papers were either destroyed or, haphazard, lost. Not until 1964 was he rehabilitated and there was a public celebration of his genius.

Letters written to his first family who were in Brussels and Paris have been recovered; also stories lost in periodicals or in salvaged manuscripts. Few have yet appeared in Russia or in translation. It is the same old stupid Soviet tale. The MacAndrew edition contains his letters and two early stories, including the famous 'My First Fee': the Max Hayward edition which first appeared in 1969 also contains early work like 'An Evening at the Empress's' and 'The Chinaman', and the texts of a long interview, and of the speeches made in 1964 by Ehrenburg, Paustovsky, Nikulin and Munblit. The Paustovsky piece supplements the fine portrait in Babel's *Years of Hope* and is a valuable and intimate account of his habits as a writer in the early days. He and Paustovsky belonged to the very talented group who began to write in Odessa in the terrible period of the Civil War. In spite of biographical criticisms made by Nathalie Babel, the edition of her father's stories introduced by Lionel Trilling in 1955 is important.

The subjects of a very large number of Babel's stories are primitive and direct. The war and the expropriations have turned the peasants on the Asiatic border into murderers, looters, and bandits; the new government forces are as ruthless in getting a new regime set up. Babel's prose is sharp and laconic. There is little comment. And yet within the fatalism of the tales there is the unmistakable Jewish humanity; sometimes the Jewish humour and fantasy – what one can only call the irony of recognition: the recognition of the manly or womanly essence of each briefly elicited character. Babel had a master in Gorki, but his deeper masters were Gogol and Maupassant: Gogol for the imaginative richness, Maupassant for detachment, economy, and devilish skill. Eventually Babel was to find Maupassant cold. What I think Babel meant was that the Frenchman was *outside*, whereas all Babel's characters carry some grain of the presence of Russia, the self being a fragment of the land's fatality. One says, as one sees the Kulak kill his horse rather than let it go to the Cheka people when he is turned out, when one sees him become a legend as a bandit, and when he is run to earth and killed in a pit: 'Yes, that is how it was. It was the end of an epoch, dreadful.' One has seen the rage of a lifetime.

As an artist, Babel describes himself in 'My First Fee':

From childhood all the strength of my being had been devoted to the invention of tales, plays and stories – thousands of them. They lay on my heart like toads on a stone. I was possessed by devilish pride and did not want to write them down prematurely.

His early idea was to 'dress them in beautiful clothes' and he could write, for example:

The flowering acacias along the streets began to moan in a low, faltering voice.

Later, in his innumerable re-writings (so that one very short tale might be drained from dozens of versions as long as a novel), his aim was to cut

[17]

and cut and cut. He was tormented by the amount of words and inventions inside himself.

On the other hand, occasionally he expanded an early version. 'My First Fee' has an early laconic version called 'Answer to an Inquiry', which contains one of those brief asides which are a remarkable but traditional part of his art – an item in a prostitute's room:

> In a small glass bowl of milky liquid flies are dying – each in his own way.

and, although the end is sharper in the first version, the second and longer one is richer. The boy's lying tale is now really fantastic; and the symbol for describing the sexual act is more truthful than anything by contemporary masturbators:

> Now tell me, I should like to ask you: have you ever seen a village carpenter helping his mate to build a house? Have you seen how thick and fast and gaily the shavings fly as they plane a beam together? That night this thirty-year-old woman taught me all the tricks of her trade.

In story after story Babel worked until he hit upon the symbol that turns it from anecdote into five minutes of life. He was not a novelist. By 1937 he was being semi-officially questioned about not writing on a large scale like Tolstoy or the very *bien vu* Sholokhov. It was being insinuated that he was idle and not pulling his weight. Poor devil! Short story writers are poets. Babel could not but be opposed to the clichés of Socialist Realism and particularly to the rhetorical magazine prose it had led to. He was also asked why he wrote of the exceptional rather than the typical, and one knows what Stalinism meant by 'typical': the middlebrow ideal. He replied with Goethe's simple definition of the *novella*: it is a story about an unusual occurrence. And he went on – the interview appears verbatim in Hayward's volume:

> ... Tolstoy was able to describe what happened to him minute by minute, he remembered it all, whereas I, evidently, only have it in me to describe the most interesting five minutes I've experienced in twenty-four hours.

[18]

He was opposed to the short story as a condensed novel. The short story is an insight.

Babel, as Ehrenburg said in his speech at the celebration in 1964, 'was formed by the Revolution'. The struggle between order and anarchy nourished him, not in a thinking or philosophical way, but instantly in terms of people and events seen with the naked eye. His official work enabled him to travel restlessly. He was eager for that, but he also hid where people could not get at him; like many famous writers in Russia and the West he was overworked in the public interest. His curiosity was eccentric and endearing. In Odessa he used to treat people or pay them to get the story of their first love. In Paris he used to pay girls to talk to him. One of his favourite questions to a lady was, 'Can I see what you have got in your handbag?'

The *Letters*, edited by Babel's daughter, are moving in their unconscious self-portrait of the anxious and worried Jew, minutely concerned about the daily life of the family from whom he was separated.

> I have already learned Natasha's school report by heart and am in dire need of new spiritual nourishment. I would like very much to know how Grisha is doing, whether he is working and whether he 'is making progresses' as a certain Jewish woman in Odessa used to say.

One can see that he was a self-burdened man who could not resist more burdens, passing from euphoria to gloom:

> I've gone completely cracked with my thirst for 'work'. I want to work every hour of my life.

His last recorded utterance was in 1939, when the police came for him. He was not alarmed – one imagines him never alarmed – the mild round face, with the strong out-of-date steel-rimmed glasses, smiled. All he said was 'I was not given time to finish'. It might be the last abrupt sentence of any of his stories.

Simone de Beauvoir

GROWING OLD

Simone de Beauvoir is one of those writers who dig and dig until they pile up the monumental. Faced by the stretches of dead wasteland in ourselves and our society, in which we dump our unsolved or evaded problems, she settles down to an exhaustive sifting and then rebuilds. She is sometimes portentous, and rarely witty; but her feelings are strong and she is unremitting in her concern. Her present object is to analyse our attitudes to old age. After dealing with the biology of the inevitable decline of the tissues and muscles, she moves on to the behaviour of a few primitive societies; next, period by period, from the Greeks and Romans to today; and then to old age as we know it in everyday life. She draws on the words and lives of many rancorous writers, painters, scientists, and musicians who, privileged by their vocations, have closely observed the change that old age has brought to them. Her object is to break the conspiracy of silence on a subject that has become privately and publicly taboo in the advanced countries which are governed by the values of profit-making capitalism.

The fact is that in this century traditional concepts of old age have lost their meaning: socially, old age has become the scrap heap. The irony is that the percentage of elderly people in the wealthier and more advanced countries has enormously increased since the beginning of the century. All but a few are forced to end what sentimental liars have called 'the golden years' on declining means among the middle class, and in poverty with little remedy among the workers. The affluent society is strictly for the under-fifties.

The fact that for the last fifteen or twenty years of his life a man should be no more than a reject, a piece of scrap, reveals the failure of our

[20]

civilization: if we were to look upon the old as human beings, with a human life behind them, and not as so many walking corpses, this obvious truth would move us profoundly.

And she reminds us of the Grimms' story: a peasant makes his father eat out of a small wooden trough, apart from the rest of the family. One day he finds his son fitting little boards together. 'It's for you when you are old,' says the child. At once the grandfather is given back his place in the family. But the Grimms' family home cannot survive in urban industrial life. The boy's father is liable to lose his job today, and when he applies to Situations Vacant he will find that 'no one over forty need apply'; he is many years away from his retirement pension and will certainly be unable to support either son or grandfather.

If one can think of thousands of exceptions to this threat, it hangs imminently over a large section of the working classes and has begun to affect the white-collar worker. First one is disqualified, then one moves on to the segregated condition of the old. All governments are plagued by what the machine or, rather, what the policy that runs the machine is doing; and in Western Europe, Scandinavia, and the United States – among the capitalist countries – there has been a great deal of research and some action which Simone de Beauvoir examines. Scandinavia, with few political difficulties to deal with and very drastic taxation, has easily done the best: the community is small enough to be coherent. It is hard to follow the regulations and statistics provided for the other countries: one can only say that good intentions are marred by meanness. The state puts the economy first and the economy is directed to maniacal productiveness.

One would have expected a writer with a Marxist turn of mind to make the communist practices clearer and, above all, more living than they appear here. One is obviously better off in these countries if one belongs to the Party, and production is still the God. One cannot tell in any country how many of the aged like being institutionalised and how many hate it, or what has been lost and what gained. I have seen many 'old folks' communities in many countries, and what is depressing about them is the unnatural sight of people living entirely and perforce among

[21]

people of their own age. One is in an organised ante-chamber for the dying or in the stiff, lifeless rooms of a doll's house. And the smell of old age pervades.

I do not think that Simone de Beauvoir's examination of primitive societies adds much more than exotic spice to the subject, though it is interesting that settled tribes behave on the whole better to the old than nomads do. Among the nomads the legs of the old cannot keep up, and they are often left behind or deliberately exposed to death. The elderly Fangs accept their fate and even joke about it. They take it to be natural that their heirs should get rid of them; sometimes they ask to be burned alive and go out in a blaze. The Hottentots admire the old, but hate the senile, who are sent off to starve, though with a great ritual feast of the tribe to send them on their way. Ceremonial politeness is at least a recognition that a man's dignity lies in his role – a concept that has vanished in the impersonal life we live nowadays, though one can observe it in the slums of Naples – and also, of course, it helps against magic, which, in our terms, means the retribution we ourselves invent.

We are becoming closer to the nomads, I think, simply because modern economic life forces us to be mobile; we move on from one exhausted hunting ground to another conveniently like it; the family, once the shelter of the old, is scattered. One certain thing primitive life shows: the old are better off in rich societies, but not rich societies like ours, where the wealth depends on each being out for himself.

The most urgent part of Simone de Beauvoir's survey is concerned with retirement, the modern nightmare. Only worn-out manual workers or people with ruined health look forward to it. The retirement forced on most people today is the real error of our industrial ethos, and it is made worse by the low pensions that rob the man or the woman of the rewards of their long labour and status. The white-collar worker adapts himself more easily than the labourer. Only the wealthy can assure themselves, when they are kicked out, of a pension that is close to their real salary, for neither the work nor the pay of the worker changes very much in the course of a lifetime.

The real shock lies in being disqualified. Some recover, others fall into poor health and listlessness when work stops. In all countries a very large proportion of the retired men simply hang about the house, particularly in America. An English woman said of her husband when he retired:

'That was a day to remember! He cried and the children cried too.' And the husband went on: 'I didn't know what to do any more. It was like when you're put in chokey in the army. I just sit staring at these four walls, that's all. Before, I used to go out with my mates on Saturday evening, or with my sons-in-law. I can't do that any more. I'm like a pauper. I haven't got a pound-note in my pocket . . . What I give my wife doesn't amount to anything . . . I'm ashamed.'

Another wife said of her husband: 'It's murder, having him in the house. He worries about what you're doing – and he's always asking questions.' One asked permission to cut the bread.

There is a long list in this book of these despondent stories from France and America as well. A good deal depends on whether those who retired were optimists or pessimists; but in general, those who did not dream of leisure are better off. Florida and the Mediterranean deceive – the latter is found to be bad for rheumatism and rents are too high – but the experience at Prairie City in the United States is that people who go on working have 'a much higher *tonus*' than the retired and their recreations are richer. And, to relieve the gloomy picture, there is a group of Burgundian bicyclists; their average age was eighty-six and activity kept them in spanking health. Many worked full time in their regular jobs, the rest found secondary occupations and devoted themselves to bicycling, walking, shooting and reading. They were ordinary men far above the intellectual level of their neighbours.

It is Mlle de Beauvoir's argument that a society like ours, which treats people as material instead of treating them as men and women, prepares its working population for boredom by maiming at the outset, but I have known many old coal miners, especially in Wales and in the North of England, of whom this was certainly not true fifteen years ago. Indeed, elsewhere in industrial England, wherever a trade was well-rooted and the community long established (as it often is), one could see that the body was aged but the communal pride and spirit were rich. In the new

generation of huge cities like London the maiming may have begun –
except in pockets like Bermondsey or among dock workers – but from
this one deduces that, education or no education, it is the clan or
community that is the real educator and the genuine source of a sustaining
culture. In so far as it breaks up real communities the new capitalism is
antihuman. It standardises the nomad.

Simone de Beauvoir is on more certain ground when she writes of old
age as it affects us privately. There *is* a conspiracy to make us believe
that the old are different from ourselves. Their passions, their sexuality,
their needs are intensified by the discovery that all time does not stretch
before them. Their angers and jealousies are notoriously fierce although
the range is narrower. As she says, there is a return not to second
childhood but to something like the wilfulness of children, and if old
people are strange it is because, as Victor Hugo and the Greek tragedians
saw, there is a psychological reconnection with the fantasies of childhood
and adolescence. Both children and the old live on the fringes of the adult
world and are therefore often mocked.

If life is tragic, society takes the view of comedy: the sexuality of old
people is frequently laughed at or censured, for there is an interested
reluctance in accepting that the old are like ourselves. Goethe's family
raged against his love for a very young girl when he was in his seventies
– they were afraid of losing their inheritance. The mocking of old men
and women in their antics with people younger than themselves or with
one another is natural for, like all satire, it aims at that part of ourselves
that hates what we find in ourselves: the comedy of disgust is as much a
purgation as tragedy is, and has the virtue of reconciliation. I am not as
shocked as Mlle de Beauvoir is by the grotesque ballet of old women
lifting up their skirts and pretending to be young, for the old are often
used to their own half-admiring self-mockery. It is even a strength, as
she indeed says about Picasso's pictures of himself as the monkeyish
dwarf man pleading and fawning before a beautiful young girl: he is
so sure of his strength that he is able to play with any situation in his
life.

To censure elderly sexuality is to forget that in those who have had a
rich sexual life, it will be prolonged. And it is at the heart of the creative

imagination, whether in artists or in the ordinary man. What is difficult
for the old is sexual loneliness. It is much worse for older women than
for men, though I cannot agree with Mlle de Beauvoir that no one speaks
of 'a beautiful old woman'. In any case, instinctive sexual attraction
may not depend on beauty at all. A voice, for example, is as potent as a
body.

These chapters on sex are very valuable, but we have to return to the
dour fact that old age is a parody of life: 'The vast majority of mankind
look upon the coming of old age with sorrow or rebellion. It fills them
with more aversion than death itself.' Emile de Faguet wrote, 'Old age is
a perpetual play that a man acts in order to deceive others and himself
and whose chief drollery lies in the fact that he acts badly.' Great men
and women may turn upon their own achievements, as Michelangelo did
when he denounced his own sculptures as puppets. There is only one
solution, Mlle de Beauvoir says: 'In spite of the moralists' opinion to the
contrary, in old age, we should wish still to have passions strong enough
to prevent us turning in upon ourselves. One's life has value so long as
one attributes value to the life of others, by means of love, friendship,
indignation, compassion.' It is not a good way of preparing for old age
to brood on the money one is setting aside, on hobbies, and on one's
place of retirement.

It is strange that Mlle de Beauvoir gives less attention to women in
this book than to men. Certainly she quotes Mme de Sévigné at length
and speaks of one or two others, but one can think of many more
signal figures. I do not believe that women have been more silent than
Chateaubriand, Hugo, Goethe, Tolstoy and Proust or many others whose
cases she examines. It is true that women have been reserved about their
emotional and sexual lives, but in all human beings of strong creative
ability there is what may be called an overflow of vitality. There is a
marked literary bent to Mlle de Beauvoir's mind, which is fortunate,
because writers, painters, and musicians have had few reserves about
their sensations as old people. Painters and musicians do better on the
whole than writers, or at any rate better than novelists, in keeping, and
indeed putting new life into, their talents. The failure of invention in
novelists is probably due to the fact that memory overcrowds their minds,

as it does the ageing minds of most of us; it suffocates the power of fantasy from which the novel springs.

All the same, it is to the novelists we must turn for the most intimate accounts of old age. Two seem to me outstanding: Italo Svevo's *Confessions of Zeno* with its astonishing portrait of Zeno's ageing father, a description which weaves clinical observation and profound imaginative sympathy together. He is dispassionate and tender, yet intellectually alert. Italo Svevo was fitted for this by his comic genius and his fervid interest in illness: life is a sickness, he said, that only death will cure, and the old know well how to mock. This cleared the ground of all conventional sentiment and morbidity at the outset and freed him to see the life of the aged in their own affronted sense of time as past and present mingled. I imagine Svevo would be too wayward for Mlle de Beauvoir – but wilfulness, after all, is one of the privileges and weapons of old age. It was Bertrand Russell in his nineties who sat down on the pavement at the CND protest in Whitehall saying, 'I am not prepared to be tolerated much longer.'

The second novel is one Mlle de Beauvoir does go into at length: *The Golovlevs* of Saltykov-Shchedrin, which is unsurpassed in its portrait of the changing mind of a woman who passes from the bustling despotism of middle age to the muddle of timeless daydreaming and the dozing frights of old age.

> She lived as though she took no personal share in existence... The weaker she grew, the louder was the voice of her desire to live... Earlier she had been afraid of death; now she seemed to have forgotten it entirely. She longed for all those things she had deprived herself of... Greed, gossip, and a self-seeking pliability developed in her with astonishing speed... The transition from cantankerous despotism to submissive flattery was no more than a question of time...

These are bleak quotations which do not bring out the real reason for the care and fullness of the portrait: this springs from the time sense of the Russian novelists of the nineteenth century – the sense of dwelling in the day itself, in the minutes that trickle through the fields or the empty room. That is precisely what the time-scale of advanced old age is: a life moving a day at a time, giddy with memory, waking with violence and fright, appeased by drowsiness and with strange austerity raising its startled head out of confusion.

With one exception the Golovlev family is closer to our subject than other variations on the theme of Lear (Mlle de Beauvoir thinks Lear may conceivably have come into Shakespeare's head when he looked at the breakdown of the manorial system under the Tudors, when unemployment and beggary spread everywhere). The exception is in the work of Samuel Beckett. His writing shows how artists are more sensitive to the burning theme that is hidden or repressed in any given period than the sociologists or reformers are. And indeed see it sooner.

Beckett is not moved by meliorist ideas but presents his old men and women as creatures who have entered a culture of frenzy, complete in itself, with its own rage of inquiry, its feverish speed of acute and changing sensation. They are at war not with death but with their own vitality. His old people are agonised by the life force that prevents them from dying. 'What tedium!' cries his Molloy, continuously, contemptuously. Beckett joins those writers who reject the idea of serenity with the frightful hilarity of people forced to survive. His fever is different from the fever of Chateaubriand's eloquent self-loathing, but both contain their truth and illumination: when we recognise the inevitable, we are strengthened to bear it or (more important in a selfish society that values long life) to endure it in others.

The social aspect is one thing, but the private is another. A thousand considerations of temperament, upbringing, and chance make generalisation impossible. Some people are born older than others and become young late in life. If we are not struck by mortal disease many of us in our seventies nowadays feel little different from what we were at fifty – though this may be a delusion – except that we now know time is shorter. If by luck of vocation or temperament we are incurably active we have little time to think of our decline. But our sense of the mysteriousness of life becomes sharper and we are jarred by the death of friends, as if by the sound of a harsh forgotten chord. If we are vain of our survival we now discover a more piercing grief, for the dead have taken away a part of ourselves. Indeed it might be said that what the old learn at last is how to grieve.

We all have known intimately men and women of all social classes in their eighties and nineties who are incredibly clear in mind and vibrating with life. How much depends on our tonnage of vitality! The only thing to be said is that these old people have usually placed themselves outside the system. They have not been worn out by others; and if they have their aches and pains, they have added to their lives by increasing their work and not by rest. Perhaps they were born unresting.

Gerald Brenan

THE SAYINGS OF DON GERALDO

There is a moment in the old age of a writer when he finds the prospect of one more long haul in prose intimidating and when he claims the right to make utterances. We grow tired of seeing our experience choked by the vegetation in our sentences. We opt for the pithy, the personal, and the unapologetic. For years we have had a crowd of random thoughts waiting on our doorstep, orphans or foundlings of the mind that we have not adopted; the moment of the aphorism, the epigram, the clinching quotation has come. So, in his eighties, Gerald Brenan has sat in his Spanish house, ignoring the fame that has gathered around him as the unique interpreter of Spanish history, politics, and literature, his energetic past as a sort of scholar-gypsy in Europe, Morocco, his previous hopes as a poet and novelist, and his interest as a confessional biographer, and has set about polishing his *pensées* in this miscellany which he has called dismissively *Thoughts in a Dry Season*. ('Dry' is the wrong word: the juices are very active in him.)

Brenan has always been a man of vast reading in many languages, interested in everything from religion, politics, literature, men, women, animals, down to flowers, trees, birds, and insects: he has lived for inquiry and discovery. Although he left school young and is innocent of the university, he cannot be called an autodidact. Greek and Latin came easily to him, he is not a dogmatic 'knower' but, as he says, a 'learner', and he has had the advantage of rarely having reviewed a book or given a lecture. A Chair has not allured him. None of his sayings is therefore a regurgitation. He confesses to having kept a commonplace book earlier in his life, but he did not keep it up. His only regret is that the exigencies of modern publishing have made him cut out his longer reflections on

[29]

history, philosophy, politics, and the phases of the revolution we are now passing through and which have been his passionate preoccupation since, I suppose, the Spanish Civil War.

Since Brenan, or Don Geraldo as the Spaniards call him, has been my closest friend for the last forty years, I cannot look at the present volume with detachment. I have sat by his blazing wood fire in his Spanish house listening to him talk this book into existence. I see and hear him rather than read it. The tall man whose glasses flash as if he were sending out signals, as he slippers about the room talking fast and softly while he looks above my head into a vast distance, or looks down suddenly as if puzzled by my existence, pops up between the lines of the printed page.

He is an egoist, a performer, who invites one into the upper air of his fantasies and insights. He is one of those excited conversationalists who at once define and transform the people, places, and ideas that have set them off. If he is an encyclopaedia, it is an encyclopaedia that has wings. He will punctuate his talk with the most elegant of smoker's coughs and the most enticing of suggestions or gossipy innuendo. I have often wished I could transcribe his manner of conversation, his sudden darts into some preposterous item of sexual news, his pleasant malice, the jokes that enliven the quirks of learning and his powers of generalisation, but the thing escapes me. But now, in the epigrams and discursive entries in this book, I hear his voice.

How does Brenan talk, what is his manner? Here it all is. This is Brenan, any day, on his terrace or by the fire or talking his way up Spanish paths, passing from village to village, switching, for example, from the idea that no village loves the next village, but only the next village but one, and that this may have its roots in Arab habit, to expounding on the cultivation of plants, the habits of birds, the moral and social influences of architecture, the problems of abstract art, T. S. Eliot's deficiency in historical sense, the nature of pretty girls, the ups and downs of sexual life, the phases of marriage, the patterns of theology, the difference between the nature of the poet and the prose writer, the differing formalities of the Mediterranean, the northern European, the Muslim, and the American cultures and their historical causes. Things are things and events are events, and he knows all about them, but they suddenly take off and become ideas and then become part of the flow of historic instances before they drop into some comical anecdote.

He has arranged his utterances in groups about life, love, marriage, death, religion, art and architecture, literature, writing, people, Nature, places, introspection, and dreams. He has invented a terse Chinese sage, Ying Chü. In his talking life these matters will run from one to another and we shall have scarcely time to agree or disagree. Here I shall note varieties in his manner, remembering that what may sound dogmatic and like a sharp military order – for there is something of the curt soldier in him – is really put forward as a question he invites us to dispute.

> Poverty is a great educator. Those who have never known it lack something.

> Most of our personal opinions lie on the board like iron filings. But pass the magnet of a strong emotion over them and they will change overnight and point in the opposite direction.

On love:

> Some girls only fall in love with ugly men. These are the girls who when they were children preferred golliwogs to dolls.

Love and admiration often precede sexual attraction and may even exclude it. Think of Stendhal and the fiasco. The following is a real Geraldo-ism:

> But women also have their problems. Thus making love to a girl for the first time can be like going into a dark room and fumbling for the electric switch. Only when a man has found it will the light come full on.

Marriage:

> In a happy marriage it is the wife who provides the climate, the husband the landscape.

On religion he is a moderate sceptic. He does not care for utilitarianism. He is not a humanist because he does not feel 'Man is a sufficiently noble animal to be given absolute power over his destiny.' He needs authority:

[31]

What authority I do not know, but my need has made me a fellow traveller of the religious, though I shall get out of their bus several stations before the end.

(He is close to Montaigne. Above all he admires Montaigne's prose, but 'not in translation').

The paintings that move him most are those that express a moment in time when things seem to be arrested and made to stand still.

I am not drawn to Rubens because in his paintings every little detail is on the move. Nothing has weight, there is no rest for the mind, one thinks chiefly of the skill and mastery.

On painting, he passes from the *pensée* to the essay, but the *pensée* punctuates the essay. On the abstract painters:

there is no struggle in their canvases, no tension – only choices and hesitations.

Yet the works of the American abstract expressionists

surge up from some deep layer on the borders of the unconscious and make a strong emotional impression.

The essay goes on to architecture –

Modern States [being strictly utilitarian] are the natural enemies of good architecture.

– and an analysis of the Romanesque, the Gothic, and the Byzantine, and praise for the Muslims for their 'abnormal sensitivity to small variations'. These are intended to 'lull the senses', and he has a eulogy of the mosque of Adrianople. All this ends with an odd kind of aside that gives a sparkle to the learned phrases of his talk. The bishop who completed Salisbury Cathedral had been Queen Philippa's chaplain, a dwarf who was notoriously impotent. He built the finest spire in England.

The entries become longer when he moves to literature. He looks at Stendhal ('an amateur in a nation of professionals'), Balzac, Flaubert, Henry James, Quevedo, Italo Svevo – a talking author very close to him, indeed I often confuse my friend with him – Jane Austen and even P. G.

Wodehouse, Góngora and many other poets, and each paragraph contains a startling *apercu*. These pages are too long to quote but I have heard many of them thrown off in high moments of his talk where they were as precise as they are in print; his conversation has the glancing quality of something rapt and yet prolonged. His afterthoughts are sudden:

> Who, for example, among English writers of talent could have written a serious poem on dentifrice, as Apuleius did, except Nabokov? And in their use of erotic subjects for unerotic ends they are also similar.

Or:

> The cliché is dead poetry. English, being the language of an imaginative race, abounds in clichés, so that English literature is always in danger of being poisoned by its own secretions.

Whereas French writing – until 'Sartre eroded the language' – relied on the precision of its syntax. All the same, clichés,

> if well chosen, provide a rest for the mind and give a more leisurely movement to the sentence . . . A good deal can be done by words that are vague and plastic: consider the use that Vergil makes of the word *res*.

So one listens to Brenan's talk for its vivacity and for the extraordinary breadth of its interests. In one section he amuses himself by bringing in his imaginary Chinese sage to whom modern rulers, from Hitler onward, come to ask advice. The troubled Nixon asks whether there is any chance of being born again in another life in which he could fulfil his potentialities. The sage reminds him that if he is reborn he will find that billions of others will be reborn – 'including all your compatriots' – and suggests he will cease to be tormented by this craving for immortality if he reflects on this, before breakfast.

As for himself, there are discreet revelations: he has the writer's shame before his own writing. Out of dullness he wakes up when he gets to his desk, but cannot believe that he is the 'I' who has written and is praised. Modesty? No, he says, conceit. Fog surrounds him: only intuition can give access to the vague shapes he discerns in the fog. All his remarks

[33]

on nature – on the toad, the snail, insects, and birds – are delightful to hear. He is a connoisseur of the distribution of the olive. To walk with him is to see creatures, trees, rocks, and soils come to life, not only because he knows so much, but because what he knows comes lightly to his tongue. A bore would have stunned us with more information. He does not inform: he incites. There is no melancholy in this Jacques:

> Rain, rain, rain. It brings out all the scents – roses, heliotrope, lemon leaves, loquat flowers, freesias, but subduing them a little and mixing them with the smell of the wet earth. This garden is where I should like to live if I were blind, because in its soft air the sounds as well as the scents have a soothing and memory-provoking quality. Ordinarily the senses take in too much. One would better enjoy using one's eyes if they recorded fewer things, because the less clearly objects are defined, the greater is the charge of emotional associations they carry.

Brenan ends by cursing the critics of poetry who insist on 'explicating'. He is no sentimentalist. He is always exacting. Be careful: if he is drawing his portrait he may be drawing yours. It will be sharp and yet you will be enlarged by his fantasy. Thousands of Malagueños came to his funeral when lately he died.

Robert Browning

PIONEER

In the last twenty-five years the cloak of legend – the cloak of the Red Cross Knight – has been twitched from the shoulders of Robert Browning. His romance no longer hides him; rather, it deepens the complexity of his double character; and his tortuous achievement as a dramatic or novelistic poet becomes more forceful in our eyes. His two new biographers – Park Honan has completed the biographical study cut short by William Irvine's death – are polished writers and they concede a great deal to Betty Miller's arguments of the 1950s, when, looking again at the famous elopement from Wimpole Street, she saw the Perseus–Andromeda situation was reversible: Andromeda also rescued Perseus.

There is nothing like the sickroom for building up the will and strengthening the mind, and Perseus was not quite the dominant figure the victim of Mr Barrett hankered after. In fact two invalids – and even two victims of the colonial slave trade – had found each other; or two histrionics, one successful at that time and the other not. (No modern biographer has accepted Miss Mitford's tough, spinsterly view that Browning was a long-haired, effeminate, climbing dandy who, living unscrupulously off his parents into his late thirties, was out to float on Miss Barrett's fame and money. Down-to-earth women like Miss Mitford are rarely good judges.) If we are going in for malice we prefer Miss Barrett's rival suitor who offered the typical gem of English suburban snobbery when he called Browning the 'New Cross Knight', thus pushing the Browning family out of genteel Camberwell to within close sight of the Surrey Docks.

It is very extraordinary that the elder Barrett and the elder Browning had the closest connection with the slave plantations, the former owing his personal fortune to them, the latter, in a clerkly manner, being sent out to St Kitts as a young man. The gentle bookworm came back quickly, shattered by the horrors he had seen. A bit of an artist, he would be caught doodling horrifying human heads in black and red ink, working off memories too awful to speak of. A meek, poorish clerk in the Bank of England, he was a childish bibliophile, a mild Voltairean, ruled by a sweet but sternly religious wife. She was of modest Scottish and German stock and – as surely as Mrs Ruskin – she knew she had given birth to a genius and was determined not to let his soul out of her command; in time, invalidism became one of *her* weapons.

One mustn't put it like this, for the boy adored her; he flourished like an ambitious mushroom in his happy prison. Only one part was mushroom; the other was restless, noisy and demanding. The mother's boy was handsome and delicate; for thirty-odd years he slept in the room next to his mother's and the door was always left open in case he or she should call. Elizabeth Barrett's door opened on her father's. Together Robert Browning and his mother had headaches and backaches and wondered at the felicity of it.

The boy refused to go to school or university after the age of fourteen, was tutored but read his way through six thousand learned books, listened to music; and got up erudite charades. Father and son re-enacted things like the siege of Troy, drawing on the furniture for battlements. The Browning cottage (Irvine writes) was a thick interior epidermis of epics, tragedies, biographies, tales, miscellanies, so that the family lived in a kind of intestine. No wonder the boy grew up to spend a lifetime turning dictionaries and encyclopaedias in French and Italian into poetry: the privacies of London suburbia have traditionally been rich in sedentary fancy. In the Brownings there seems to have been a delight in congesting the intellect and the emotions.

At twenty, the young Browning proudly refused to clerk or go into the law and decided to live by writing epics of introspection, and the parents – living on £257 a year – submitted and supported him. They even raked up money to send him to Italy and Russia. He dressed with elegance and never left the house without white gloves: they were a lifelong obsession. Why? Unclean, unclean? Here we must be cautious.

The one violent disturbance in his life was his contact with the atheism of Shelley. Christian respectability had long replaced the ideas of the French Revolution and Mrs Browning drove him to recant; the guilt attached to this surrender lasted his life. Surely this has nothing to do with gloves, but Irvine takes the plunge:

> . . . Robert's zealous regard for gloves – old or new – astonished even his contemporaries. The need to conceal his hands seems to have been one feature of that larger, more intricate need to resort to camouflage in his writing; to conceal the unresolved conflicts in his own personality from the world's eye, and to live almost comfortably and respectably with his mother's religion and Shelley's poetry. Even the most autobiographical passages in darkest *Sordello* suggest that he could not bear to examine his own deepest loyalties too closely or directly.

But one remembers Balzac's passion for gloves. One surely does not argue that the English took to carrying umbrellas because they were seeking psychological shelter. Surely the glove was no more than an intimate token of elegance and sentiment in European life, an item of dandyish fastidiousness also. A naval officer was so taken by the young Browning on the voyage from London to Venice that he kept a pair of his gloves as a remembrance. At most Browning was displaying the histrionic vanity that Jung associates with introverts. The boisterous Browning was a deeply introverted and happy prisoner of his childhood, perhaps all his life. If his conflicts were insoluble, they were the source of his actor-like gift for dressing up and vicariously living in others.

The most enlightening passages in the present biography are the critical ones which go into this and into the obscurities of Browning's writings. On the Wimpole Street romance, the authors follow the story sensibly; but the courtship is really much better read in the recent Elvan Kintner edition of the letters, which bring out the important and deeply Browning-esque point that the two parties are really four – their epistolary and real selves – who seem to be trying to get into a future story by Henry James. The irony was that Elizabeth Barrett sought an autocrat and Browning obstinately wanted to be ruled: he for the goddess in her, not she for the

[37]

god in him. In their letters, both are cleverer – one guesses – than in life.

As for Browning's 'semantic stutter', there have been many theories about the cause. Irregular education, no logical training, is one. The chaos created by voracious and random reading; the tumbling in of images from constant listening to music; a sort of congestion of ideas in a mind isolated within a peculiar family, a conceit of originality very common in narrow religious sects; the egotism of such an isolation – these explanations have been advanced. There is the obvious influence of Carlyle: more here than meets the eye, for Mrs Browning was of Scottish and German stock and one suspects the sweet domestic lady could become flinty and ablaze with Biblical metaphor and even German grotesque if, say, the subject of Shelley and atheism came up.

But another explanation seems to me overruling: the imprisoned intro-vert was a violent man, acting out violent Calvinist fantasies in words; he was by nature, though not by gift, a man of the theatre. His words, his inverted phrases, his telescopings, his grotesqueries, are syntax as a stage cast: words are players. It is important that he spent many years writing tragedies and melodramas in verse in the hope that Macready would produce them. Of all the English poets of the nineteenth century Browning seemed the most likely to succeed on the stage; he was determined on it. But, his biographers say:

> From first to last, Browning attempted to depict, as he said in the original preface to *Strafford*, 'Action in Character, rather than Character in Action.' . . . As his venture grew desperate, he turned from history to romance and violence, but action continued – ever more glaringly – to be an ironic irrelevance to character . . . He treated the theatre as a gigantic laboratory . . . Some lessons he could not learn. Browning was fascinated by motives, but seemed scarcely interested in how motives produced action or how one action must be linked logically and psychologically with another. He could depict character in isolation – even at a moment of crisis – but he could not easily bring one character into dynamic relation with another.

In short his gifts were those of the novelist or the poet of monologue. There is a proliferation of brilliant detail, so that the small things and psychological dilemmas become more dramatic than the main drama. He adopts the point of view of characters unlike himself, and this putting on of another's voice and life depends on a certain bouncing abruptness and on an acute sense of the mind's sensations. There is a double take: the poet is both outside and inside the husband in these lines from *The Ring and the Book*:

> Up he jumps.
> Back to mind come those scratchings at the grange,
> Prints of the paw about the outhouse; rife
> In his head at once again are word and wink,
> *Mum* here and *budget* there, the smell o' the fox,
> The musk o' the gallant.
> 'Friends, there's falseness here!'

Difficult rather than obscure, simply because deviousness and the 'impossible' perversely attracted him, Browning is one of those who, except in direct dramatic song, are travelling underground with torches of imagery in a mind that is often too continuously vivid. The effect is of broken mosaic, thought and feeling turned into broken-up things and events:

> Till sudden at the door a tap discreet,
> A visitor's premonitory cough,
> And poverty had reached him in her rounds.

The symbols 'tap', 'cough', and 'door' are stronger than 'poverty' because exact. A stuttering demagogue, said Chesterton. A crowd of arguments, theories, casuistries, images in physical shape rush together to the point of his pen at once. Our first impressionist? Irvine points out, what one easily forgets because of Browning's originality, that he did not invent impressionism or the dramatic monologue. The most interesting suggestion is that what he does not owe to Carlyle, he owes to Burns. (Mrs Browning the elder would have been pleased to hear this.)

The Ring and the Book – despite what Henry James called its 'inordinate muchness' – *is* in advance of its time. It *does* look forward to twentieth-century impressionism, as the poetry 'deprecates itself by prose expressions ... and even by unmelodious strings of compound epithets'. Another source of difficulty is that life is embedded in a dense texture of historical reading. So much of Browning was refracted through the medium of other arts, particularly music and painting, as well as through antiquarian vestiges. Browning was tremendously a Victorian in that he was a collector; his ego also colonised history, particularly the medieval, with something of the Protestant mercantile aggression. Another excellent point is that (possibly like some ornate ham) Browning turns himself into a myth. He wrote to a prim admirer:

> We differ apparently in our conception of what gross wickedness can be effected by cultivated minds – I believe the gross*est* – all the more, by way of reaction from the enforced habit of self-denial which is the condition of men's receiving culture.

Mr Honan suggests in the later chapters that *The Ring and the Book* nevertheless marks a decline – too much of the didactic, lack of self-confidence or faith, which lead him to blare too loudly on his trumpet.

The wall between Browning's public and private selves becomes thicker as time goes by. The commonsensical and sanguine man of the world becomes stronger. He was loud and seemed more like a prosperous grocer than a great poet. Presumptuous, he was more than once inept in his relations with the adoring women who surrounded him after Elizabeth's death. Grief had left him hardened. He felt no longer. He became, as these biographers note, a sort of Richard Feverel with a System in his attitude to his son; indeed there are close resemblances in life and language, and fundamental lack of invention, with Meredith, the novelist, another adept of idealism and the grotesque.

One can suspect that as a poet Browning was drawn to Elizabeth Barrett by her remarkable facility, by the lack of confusion in her feeling, even by the easy popular spontaneous throb of her coloured verse. Invalidism had in fact matured her. One can also see that she must have been one more mother figure; in his later poems there are moments when he resents, now she is dead, that memory chains him; love and hate run close in an angered mind. Yet the chains were also a protection to a poet who seems always to have wished to mask his own life so that he could pour himself into the skins of others. In this he was undoubtedly a novelist – perhaps the earliest to move towards the twentieth century.

Bruce Chatwin

WELSH PEASANTS

After the excellent book on his travels, *In Patagonia*, it is at first surprising to find Bruce Chatwin writing a novel about the small sheep farmers at home on the hills of the Welsh Border country of England. On reflection, sheep-farming is a natural link. In the nineteenth century, as if drawn to the isolation, the rains, the snows and stern conditions they knew at home, large numbers of tough, poor and thrifty Welsh migrated to Patagonia, where they were free of the alien gaze and rule of the despised Sassenach conquerors. The people of *On the Black Hill* are part of this sturdy remnant who toiled and haggled at home. But if the novel is a watchful traveller's journey through peasant life during the first eighty years of this century, its characters are strong enough to burst the bond of local record and fortune. They are carrying with them the inner life of their race. *On the Black Hill* has been compared to works like Thomas Hardy's *The Woodlanders* or *Tess of the D'Urbervilles*, because it comes so close to the skin of its people, but the comparison is misleading. Chatwin dispenses with grand tragic plot and the theatrical use of coincidence. Above all there is no classical President of the Immortals, indifferent to human fate; there is no Victorian pessimism.

The imagination of the Border people is mythical and Biblical: it has been lit by the torrential eloquence of their dissenting preachers. (The exception among Mr Chatwin's people is an Anglican clergyman and Greek scholar who scorns the Bible and who distributes the *Odyssey* to his parishioners. He was also joint master of the local hunt and was continually called upon as the only man who could save a swarm of bees barehanded. He tipped them into hives which he compared to Athens.) The Bible people see themselves as descendants of Abraham – the man of flocks – and look upon the money-making English cities across the Border as examples of the corruption of Sodom. They see themselves as travellers to the 'Abiding City' of God.

Strangeness plainly stated is the key to the book, the mingling of outward and inner life. The story is dominated by two bachelor brothers who are identical twins. They are thrifty farmers who slave until late old age on poor mountainy land in an isolated farm originally called Ty-Cradoc – the name of Caractacus, the Welsh hero who fought the Roman invaders is still evocative in the Border country – but now known as The Vision because a country girl saw the Virgin there in the eighteenth century. Benjamin and Lewis Jones are old men who have shared the same bed and worn-out bedclothes since the death of their parents and we go back over their lives. They are normal shrewd hard-working men but they are magnetised by their likeness to each other and their awareness of each other's minds. Very important to them is that they were born of an unlikely marriage. Their father was a hot-tempered labourer who had married the educated and lonely daughter of an eccentric scholarly clergyman who had suddenly died. She had spent her childhood in India, seemingly in an Anglican mission. It is she who fights to stop her two sons from becoming village dolts. They get a little schooling – much against their father's will – but she brings them up on Shakespeare, Euripides, Hardy and – of all people – Zola – perhaps because of *La Terre*. But the Bible is still their mainstay and her education has an odd effect on them. Late in life they will eagerly turn to Giraldus Cambrensis and to Froissart's *Chronicles*. If the mother had to put up with brutality from the husband she loved and who loved her she never left him. The sons worshipped her, loved the Indian relics she brought with her and in old age slept out of piety under the worn-out coverlets she had stitched together.

When they were born the mother could not tell her sons apart and indeed throughout their lives they gazed mystified by each other. They were never to go away further than Hereford thirty miles off and once only, in 1910, to the seaside. Lewis, the elder by half an hour, was tall and stringy. At the age of eighty he could walk miles over the hills easily or wield a heavy axe all day. 'He gave off a strong smell. His head would wobble as he spoke: unless he was fumbling with his watch-chain, he had no idea what to do with his hands.' The two men would often take out their watches, not to tell the time, but to see whose watch was going faster. Lewis would say no more than 'Thank you!' or 'Very kind of you!' if anyone made a statement of fact to him. He was brilliant with sheep dogs. Benjamin grew up to be shorter, pinker and neater, rather bald with an aggressive long nose. His chief skill was delivering lambs. After their mother's death he did the cooking, the darning and the ironing, kept the accounts and, like his brother, was an extremely hard bargainer and stingy, except with their hay which he gave away to any neighbour in need, saying it was 'God's gift to the farmer'. Lewis was the restless one. Among the pictures in their home there was one of a Red Indian in his birch-bark canoe, and this, together with the memory of learning to recite Longfellow's *Hiawatha* from their mother, gave Lewis a restless desire for far-off places. He was mad about geography.

> He would pester visitors for their opinions on 'them savages in Africky'; for news of Siberia, Salonika or Sri Lanka; and when someone spoke of President Carter's failure to rescue the Teheran hostages, he folded his arms and said, decisively, 'Him should'a gone to get 'em through Odessa'.

He developed in time a fascination for air crashes and kept a record of them. At the end of his life he even took a short trip in a plane.

It was Lewis who hankered after girls – a danger to their closeness and once the cause of a violent quarrel which their mother had always feared. (There is an account, strangely close to the horse-riding seduction scene in Turgenev's *Torrents of Spring*, in which a local artist's wife seduced Lewis, having betted her husband that she would.) Benjamin guessed this at once: the twin brothers knew each other's thoughts; they could even quarrel without speaking. In middle life Lewis outraged Benjamin by buying a tractor which he thought of as a woman and wanted to give a woman's name. He worshipped it, loved its noise and thought the engine as perplexing as a woman's anatomy.

In their early childhood Benjamin was stung by a wasp but it was Lewis who cried and who showed a curious life-long power of taking his brother's pain on himself. They used each other's names. Benjamin screamed when they were separated and ran away from people who could tell them apart. They had curious games, such as standing forehead to forehead staring into each other's eyes in wonder. When their sister was born they hated her and played at having babies – their mother had to stop them; so they played at being new-born lambs – not so strange perhaps: children often play at being animals. At school when they played football, it was fatal to put them on opposite sides: Benjamin would dash across to Lewis's side. In the classroom they gave identical answers to questions. Their most agonising time came with the 1914 war, when conscription started. Lewis was allowed to go off and work on another farm: Benjamin had to join the army. Benjamin pined. He gave up washing for fear of reminding himself that – at the same moment – Lewis might be sharing someone else's towel. He hated Lewis for leaving and suspected him of 'stealing his soul'. One day, staring into the shaving mirror he watched his face growing fainter and fainter, as if the glass were eating it. Later, in the army, Benjamin deserted and was arrested. Lewis knew by the pains in his own coccyx that his brother was being beaten up in the Detention barracks.

Around the brothers are their strange neighbours, notably the Watkins family at the Rock. Watkins is a coffin-maker. The son of that family is a notorious thief who seduces his own sister. After the father's death the mother sees money in fostering the bastard children of the countryside, a bedraggled bemused collection who come and go as the years pass. As the two brothers prosper the Watkins family collapse into rural misery. There is a suicide and there are awful deaths when the farms are isolated in bad winters. We are watching strange processions of raw people as they grope their way fiercely and sometimes comically through their lives: they are neither the poeticised people of early nostalgic novels about peasant life, nor are they crude and Zolaesque. They take their open sexuality for granted. Mr Chatwin is not an erotic novelist but he does convey the ruling sexual excitement. There is a robust account of a lusty Welsh Fair where Lewis, who is after the girls, makes Benjamin take a spin on the Wall of Death and Benjamin has to face the sight of the girls with their dresses flying over their faces and sees bare flesh. He staggers into the street and vomits into the gutter. After that the girls could not get Lewis away from him.

Mr Chatwin's writing is plain and direct. He has perhaps learned from the Russians 'to make it strange'. He is delicately true to changes of sky, weather and landscape and is remarkable in his power to bring human feeling to the sight by some casual action.

I find the following simple incident remarkable. Lewis has gone to see Rose Fifield who had rejected him as a lover when she was a maid at the Big House and was willingly seduced and abandoned by the son of the family. She has turned into a broken oldish woman and Lewis goes to see her out of charity because she is ill and in want; there is nothing but some jars of pickled onions in the house. She does not thank him for the food he has brought and there is little in their monosyllabic chat:

> Before leaving, he foddered her sheep which had gone a whole week without hay. He took the milk-can and promised to come back on Thursday.
>
> She clutched his hand and breathed, 'Till Thursday then?'
>
> She watched him from the bedroom window walking away along the line of hawthorns, with the sunlight passing through his legs. Five times, she wiped the condensation from the pane until the black speck vanished from view.
>
> 'It's no good,' she said out loud. 'I hate men – all of them.'

That phrase 'with the sunlight passing through his legs' is an example of Mr Chatwin's ability to catch the evanescent detail that lights not simply the act of parting but a moment in the life of the heart. He is a master of catching the day itself passing through his people. He is not a professional sorrower at the toils of the peasantry.

The modern world comes slowly in with its trippers and its week-enders, its washing machines, its cheating antique dealers who try to strip the old farmers of their treasures; but the Bible is the ruling consolation. The mythical world lives side by side with reality. The Border people live by their imagination. We shall see Theo, the Afrikaner, at a Harvest Festival reading from the Book of Revelation at the Chapel. Preaching has done something for him. With fervour he lists the jasper and jacinth, the chryso-

[46]

prase and chalcedony, without misplacing a syllable. The visiting preacher cried out that he felt he could reach out and touch the Holy City:

> [But this was] not a city like Rome or London or Babylon! Not a city of Canaan, for there was falsity in Canaan! This was the city that Abraham saw from afar . . .

The preacher is a Welsh nationalist of extreme views but, in the cautious Welsh way, 'expressed these views in so allusive a language that few of his listeners had the least idea what he was talking about'. He was (Mr Chatwin notes) wearing a suit of 'goose-shit green' and had the habit of 'cupping his hands in front of his mouth, and gave the impression of wanting to catch his previous statement and cram it back between his teeth'. Droll and yet manly he is storing his breath up, perhaps, for the moment when he would let out thunder so that Abraham would become undistinguishable from a traditional Celtic giant.

Flaubert & Turgenev

SPECTATORS

━━━━━━

What are the bonds between pairs of inveterate bachelors? For the rest of us, such men are a rare, protected species. In her introduction to *Flaubert & Turgenev: A friendship in letters*, Barbara Beaumont quotes the French critic E. M. de Vogüé: 'There can only be close friendship and solidarity between two men when their intellects have made contact.' The bond between Flaubert and Turgenev was their common belief in the primacy of art, and their innate role as spectators of events outside it. They were to be friends for seventeen years, from their forties until Flaubert died, in 1880. There was little of the attraction of opposites. The stout and bellowing Norman saw himself as a sedentary Viking and was corpulent and tall. Turgenev was dubbed 'the gentle giant' or 'amiable Barbarian' at the famous Magny dinners in Paris where they first met, and if his voice was quiet it could quickly rise to almost hysterical shrillness when he was excited. He was continually mocked for this in St Petersburg society. If giant faced giant, it is important that they seemed exotic to each other. Bald, red-faced, bourgeois Flaubert, with his oriental affectations, faced a soft, heavy man with thick white hair, the melancholy Russian landowner and aristocrat. They enormously admired each other's work. On Flaubert's side – and he flattered himself on his powers of research – there was awe before the range of Turgenev's knowledge. Turgenev seemed to have read everything of importance, 'even the darkest recess of every literature in the world'. He could speak, read and write, translate at a glance anything in French, German, and English as well as the Classics. He could declaim from Voltaire's tragedies – from Goethe, too – from memory. He was the finest of critics, and yet he could write *Fathers and Sons*, and could give himself intensely to *Salammbô* and *Madame*

Bovary. Both men loved food and wine, and talking long into the night.

If the decisive bond was of congenial minds, there was also a bond of private history. When they were younger, both men had been dominated by their mothers. Flaubert loved his mother deeply. He lived with her in Croisset. Turgenev's mother had been a barbarous and thrashing monster to her serfs and her sons, and only he, the favourite, had been able to placate her. If he hated her, he pitied her. She had been outraged when he fell under the spell of Pauline Viardot, the world-famous Spanish opera singer – 'That ugly gypsy!' she shouted. And, indeed, Pauline Viardot had enslaved and never rewarded him. If Flaubert boasted of his feats when he was free of his mother, in Paris, or his travels in North Africa, he stuck firmly (as all the French did at Magny's) to the idea that love was of passing importance to the artist. But Turgenev, himself believing that marriage was disastrous to art, declared that all his life he had been 'steeped in feminality'. No book, or anything else, had 'been able to take the place of a woman for me,' he wrote. 'How can I explain it? I find that only love produces a certain fulfilment of one's being.' He went on to tell the story of an affair with the poor miller's daughter who had refused all presents and had asked him merely for a bar of soap, so that 'she might make herself worthy of her lover's caresses'. There had been nothing in his life, he said, to compare with that moment. Flaubert, Gautier, Daudet, Sainte-Beuve, and the Goncourts were astounded. How naïve, how Russian, the gentle Barbarian was in his *aperçus*. The touching thing in the lives of the two bachelors is that they were united in their devotion to a mother figure whose Radical politics shocked Flaubert particularly – 'poor old mother Sand'. Eagerly they went to her exhausting parties at Nohant.

Of the two friends, Flaubert the hermit is the lonelier, the jealous and more demanding one. From year to year, he is begging the Russian to stay with him at Croisset, but there are Turgenev's annual trips to Russia. In France, there are his violent attacks of gout and his gadabout social life in Paris which delay him at the last minute. If he agrees to meet, he is inevitably hours late. The habit of carrying a dozen watches on his person is clearly an affectation; he has no sense of time at all. He carries them simply to amuse Pauline Viardot's children. Flaubert is convinced that the Viardots will not allow Turgenev out of their sight; he is jealous.

After all these years, to be the slave of a woman who has turned you down!

In the late sixties, there is a long separation. Turgenev leaves Paris, as it seems, for good. Viardot trouble again! Pauline Viardot's great voice has gone: she can give no more performances. She and her husband settle shrewdly in fashionable Baden, where she gives expensive lessons to the daughters of the rich and the princely. Turgenev joins them, builds a house there, and even a little theatre for her, and settles to writing *Torrents of Spring*, and his stories. Flaubert delights in the stories, picking out the exquisite sentences that Turgenev writes so easily, while he is left groaning for days over phrases of his own. Suddenly, the war of 1870 breaks out. The Germans shell Strasbourg. The Viardots are ruined and flee to London, and Turgenev joins them. Here we fear a serious rift in the friendship, for Turgenev has been distinctly pro-German. But no, for Flaubert is angry with the irresponsibility of the French government: its conduct confirms his belief in the corruption of the hated French bourgeoisie. He has suffered the humiliation of having Germans billeted in his house and admits that the sight of their helmets on his bed has angered him but says that the foreigners behaved well. Still, 'seeing my country die has made me realise that I loved it'. But he *is* distraught enough to hope that Turgenev's Russia will avenge the French defeat! Then comes the awful rioting of the Commune. 'Oh we have hard times,' Turgenev writes, 'to live through, those of us who are *born spectators.*'

The Viardots return to Paris, and Turgenev with them. There are long conversations; Turgenev continues to be late. As the years pass, there is a common cause not only in literature but in family disasters. Russia may be 'green and gold, vast, monotonous, gentle and old fashioned and terribly static', but Turgenev is in trouble with his brother, who is cheating him out of his income from the family estate. The husband of Flaubert's niece has gone bankrupt and is slyly robbing him. Flaubert writes:

Are you like me? I prefer to let myself be robbed rather than act in self-defence, it's not that I'm not interested, but it all bores and wearies me. When it's a question of money, disgust and rage seize hold of me and I go almost out of my mind.

[50]

And he goes on, 'Ah! Dear friend, how I should love to stretch out alongside you on your great haystacks.'

The letters turn to their binding enthusiasm for each other's work. The two writers examine sentences. They praise. Letters talk for them. Turgenev has done an introduction for a Russian translation of Flaubert's '*Un Coeur Simple*', but the Russian censor has banned it: there can be no possibility in Orthodox Russia of publishing the story of an old servant who has come to believe a parrot is the Holy Ghost! While Turgenev – the faster writer – has started his last novel, *Virgin Soil*, Flaubert has begun the encyclopaedic *Bouvard and Pécuchet*. Turgenev begs him, very wisely, to cut it to the length of a short satire by Voltaire or Swift, but Flaubert obstinately makes his two clowns go on to geology and archaeology, in their quixotic obsession with the quest for book-learning. 'What an abyss (a wasps' nest or a latrine) I have stuffed myself into!' he tells Turgenev. 'By the autumn you must come and stay.' Turgenev fails once more – his gout is terrible but he sends Flaubert a new Oriental dressing-gown to make up for his absence and Flaubert is ecstatic: 'This royal garment plunges me into dreams of absolutism and luxury. I should like to be naked underneath and harbour Circassian women inside it.' The two friends send each other enormous parcels of exquisite food.

Turgenev is still grappling with *Virgin Soil*, a work also too long. (If it failed in Russia, it was a huge success outside Russia and, above all, in America.) Flaubert's little fortune is vanishing. The sales of his books are small, and his friends, with Turgenev and Maupassant in the lead, attempt to get him a comfortable sinecure – a delicate matter, for the Norman is proud. He refuses to be 'a State pensioner'. In the end, he gives in. His friends call on the powerful minister Gambetta, who refuses them. The pension is reserved for the son of a politician! Turgenev's account of the interview in the corridors of power is masterly. Gambetta says merely two words as he leaves the room with his sycophants and waves the party away.

In collections of letters, the minor domestic events, the odd little details give the accidental human piquancy. Turgenev worries about Flaubert's weight and tells him to walk more. He says that when he was in prison – indeed, in solitary confinement – in Russia he had saved his own life by making four hundred and sixteen trips up and down his cell every day, achieving two kilometres in all. This was carefully calculated. He had used playing cards for counting his steps. The gadabout – 'a squirrel in a cage', as he called himself – an outsize squirrel – had his resources. Flaubert replied that five minutes after getting this advice 'I broke my leg'. This was almost true. The press got hold of the story, and he raged against the vulgarity of an age without privacy: 'I found that paragraph *very distasteful.*'

The two gourmets indulged themselves on Flaubert's fifty-eighth birthday. Soon afterward, Turgenev had to go to Moscow to attend a banquet at the inaugural celebrations for a statue of Pushkin. He knew Flaubert would not join him but begged him, 'the greatest novelist in Europe', to send a telegram, which would be read to enthusiastic public applause. He thought continually of his friend's fame. But now Flaubert is the defaulter. In his penultimate letter, he says he is 'principally indignant against Botanists. It is impossible to get them to understand a question that seems as clear as anything to me.' Turgenev replied from Russia, but the letter was delayed. His friend was dead when it arrived.

Humboldt

UNIVERSAL MAN

━━━━━━━

Alexander von Humboldt is one of the irresistible scientific brains of the late eighteenth century. Born in 1769, he died at the age of ninety, a year before the publication of the *Origin of Species*. He aimed at nothing less than universal knowledge and as an explorer he was Napoleonic: he invaded the natural sciences and remade their foundations. Napoleon himself hated and suspected this conquering intellect and commanding personality. Kings, presidents, governments and scientists consulted Humboldt obsequiously on everything from the geography of their countries to the natural resources, and he was a social idol too. As for his feats, like his climb of Chimborazo (for which he held the record in high climbing for a generation) or his disappearance for years in the forests and mountains of Venezuela, Ecuador and Peru, they appealed to the popular imagination everywhere; and though he did not discover the Humboldt current off the South American coast, it was spontaneously given his name after he had made his famous oceanographic survey there. His grand work *Cosmos*, which set out to depict in 2000 pages and in detail

> the entire material universe, all that we know of the phenomena of heaven and earth, from the nebulae of stars to the geography of mosses and granite rocks – and in a vivid style that will stimulate and elicit feeling,

defines the range of his confident and armoured nature which, like that of almost all explorers, had its strange reserves.

Well known to the general reader of the nineteenth century, Humboldt is one of those heroes of science who are inevitably superseded and become remote to all except specialists as time goes by. Douglas Botting's new popular biography reintroduces us to the career and the writings. There is, as he says, a difficulty about the latter. The man of feeling was tortured by the failure to 'elicit' it. He was an exhaustive fact-collector but in prose imagination failed him. He lacked the grace and idiosyncrasy that make great scientists like Wallace and Darwin and the self-effacing Bates delightful; and one cannot but think that he knew the private reason for this. It was strange that a man who charmed men and women with his spell-binding monologues, whose passionate spirit gave such pleasure in his friendships, should harden in writing. There is a personal mystery here which is linked with the dilemmas which set genius on its course. Douglas Botting's Life is interesting about this. He has gone to the proper sources, the text is well organised, and as a traveller in South America and Siberia, he has often found himself on Humboldt's paths. But the book does suffer from lapses into the breezy and blokey style of the broadcasting studio. Humboldt is seen 'bumping into' and 'catching up' with people; when he is nearly drowned off Cartagena we are told 'clearly it was not Humboldt's night'; in London the East India Company drop him because he is a 'hot potato'. Still, the travels have been skilfully drawn from Humboldt's narratives, and the dilemma of Humboldt's character, as he goes from success to success and rises above seemingly disastrous political setbacks, is given its dignity.

Humboldt was born with great advantages. A young aristocrat, handsome and rich, he was sure of privileged position whether he had gifts or not. (These appeared late because he was a slow learner.) But his disadvantages were serious as well. He was born into a dull provincial society – Berlin was a backward city of 140,000 people, scientific education scarcely existed, science was half-superstition: he did not even hear of botany until he was eighteen – and he was brought up by an unfeeling mother who thought little of him. The emotional check in his childhood was critical to a man of strong passions and dominant character. He turned, inevitably, to romantic friendships with men and, once feeling was aroused, the energies of will and mind were released. Women excited him, but his affections ended in wariness. One woman, the young wife of a Jewish professor who had led him to science, did dazzle him; he was almost in love with her and she became his first confessor. He revealed

[54]

to her one of his startling dreams in which men became women then turned once more into men: a dream which suggests an androgynous rather than purely homosexual nature. It is probable that he remained chaste all his life. His passionate friendships he described as 'brotherly'. They were profound and invigorating, even if they eventually led to despair when, through marriage or some other reason, they had to break. (With one couple he travelled on their honeymoon.) It may be that the curious interest in the hermaphrodite which appeared in Europe at the time of the French Revolution may have caught his mind and encouraged him; he certainly held to the political idea of the brotherhood of man with something more than intellectual conviction. What seems certain is that he turned to ambition, hard work and encyclopaedic knowledge, as Mr Botting says, to escape from the temptations of the flesh.

Sublimation, masochism or the firm shutting of the door on the private self? The dilemma was scotched by Humboldt's efficiency, his determination and his confidence in himself as a superior being. His mother had forced him into the dull life of the civil service. He chafed at it but, once there, he soon surpassed his older colleagues by his ability and leapt to the rank of Assistant Inspector of Mines. Wealth and influence helped but he now outdid anything influence expected. He went to the derelict mines of Bayreuth, documented the forgotten sixteenth-century workings and was down in the pits from four in the morning till ten at night, applying his mind to every detail. His success was spectacular. In one year the yield of gold approached what had previously taken eight years, and at half the cost. At twenty-six he was famous. His health, which had been delicate, improved and from that time on it became impervious. And he had added humanity to a far-seeing intelligence. The wretched miners needed education and protection. He started a mining school which was thronged by the men. He analysed the gases at great risk to himself, invented a form of breathing apparatus, paid for the school out of his own money and refused the State's offer to repay him, asking instead for the money to be put to creating a pension fund for the old and sick miners. The task had not only been one of applying scientific knowledge; it also came out of a determined social conscience which, in later years, made him suspect to reactionary governments. He wrote that

[55]

Steben had such a strong influence on my ideas, I worked out so many of my greatest plans there and abandoned myself so completely to feeling that I almost dread the impression it would make on me if I ever saw it again. During my stay there, especially in the autumn and winter of 1793, I was kept in a state of such nervous tension, that I could never see the lights of the cottages at Spitzberg shining through the evening mist without emotion. On this side of the ocean no place would ever seem to me its equal.

Having succeeded, he was restless and he resigned his post. He was looking for the chance of scientific travel. There was also an emotional crisis. He suffered when his love for an officer in the Prussian army was frustrated by the young man's marriage. There is evidence that he may have thought of ending his life. But his mother died, and an immense fortune came to him. He went to Paris. He hoped to go with Lord Bristol to Egypt, following Napoleon's train of scientific experts, but the war stopped that. His imagination was stirred by a meeting with Bougainville, who had sailed round the world. Then he found Bonpland, the botanist, already experienced as an explorer; after many failures they walked from Marseilles across Spain to the court of Carlos IV, and in this unlikely place their luck turned, and they were granted the royal permit to explore the resources of South America. The future course of Humboldt's life was settled.

The explorer appears: the tall, almost elegant man in the high hat, surrounded by his scientific instruments, pushing on indefatigably every day, making his notes in the forests of Venezuela, arriving at the cataracts of the Orinoco, moving to the upper Amazon and that dramatic moment when the needle of the compass turns from north to south, climbing volcanoes in Ecuador, the first to be let into the secret of the preparation of *curare* and to observe the scarcely-known value of guano as a fertiliser. He was enraged by the treatment of the Indians at the Christian missions:

To say that the savage, like the child, can be governed only by force, is merely to establish false analogies. The Indians of the Orinoco are not great children; they are as little so as the poor labourers in the east

[56]

of Europe, whom the barbarism of our feudal institutions has held in the rudest state.

He went on to the silver mines of Mexico and to the United States, where Jefferson was one of the earliest to get as much as he could out of him, for political reasons of his own, and got back to Paris after five and a half years with his fantastic collection, to become thereafter the scientific adviser to the world.

As an explorer and as a temperament, Humboldt was a man of iron, without physical weakness. Of course, he pushed himself forward and saw to it that Bonpland took second place in the fame of their South American travels – still, the egotist was naïve. He was ambitious, he monopolised, was often arrogant and bellowed, in the German way, but it did not greatly offend because of his charm. His 'love affairs' with men continued, and so did his philanderings with women.

Mr Botting's book is beautifully illustrated with excellent and out-of-the-way colour plates and drawings of the period in the best Rainbird manner. They are especially worth having in the book of a traveller, and few are well known.

Molly Keane

IRISH BEHAVIOUR

After the Treaty in the Twenties the Anglo–Irish gentry – the 'Ascendancy' as they were called – rapidly became a remnant. Some stormed out shouting insults at the receding Wicklow Hills. Those who stayed on resorted to irony; for centuries they had been a caste in decline on a poor island-within-an-island in Britain's oldest colony. They stuck to their wild passions for huntin', shootin', fishin', the turf, drink, and, above all, genealogy, as the damp rose in their fine but decaying houses. Debts and mortgages gathered around them, but they had long settled for not knowing history socially except when it presented itself in the form of family trees (sometimes done in tapestry) going back to the Normans, the Elizabethans, even to Charlemagne.

The snobbery approached, as Stendhal would have said, the Sublime. In their time this race had produced great generals, clever colonial servants, excellent playwrights, writers in prose and poetry. In these last, their particular gift lay in clear swift writing, in the unrelenting, almost militant comedy of manners or in uproarious farce. How often, in the expectant stare of their eyes, one noticed a childlike or raging innocence and the delight in mischief. Their condition was the nearest thing in Western Europe to, say, Gogol's or Turgenev's Russian landowners, and this in the ever-changing light of an often graceful landscape, and in a climate that either excited the visionary in them or drove them in on themselves.

As one who knew something of the period of Molly Keane's *Good Behaviour* I was astonished to find there no hint of the Irish 'Troubles', the Rising of 1916, the later civil war, or the toll of burned-down houses. Was this an instance of the Anglo–Irish, indeed of the general Irish habit of euphemism and evasion? What, of course, is not unreal to Molly Keane is the game of manners, the instinctive desire to keep boring reality at bay, yet to be stoical about the cost.

The Victorian and Edwardian codes stayed on far longer in southern Ireland than in England. *Good Behaviour* was less a novel than a novelised autobiography which exposes the case of Anglo–Irish women, especially in the person of the narrator, a shy, large, ungainly, horsey girl. The males, young or old, are always away, either fighting in the 1914 war or shooting and fishing or dangling after less innocent girls abroad. For the women at home sex is taboo, yet marriage is the only hope – so long as you remember that by their nature 'It's a thing men do, it's all they want to do, and you won't like it.' Love, like sex, is really a state of cease-fire. One of the rules of good behaviour is that you say nothing about *it* unless it is done by animals. The native Catholic servants, untroubled by the use of euphemism or 'place', burst with gaudy oaths to your face. They are chiefly excited by illness and death and are passionate adepts at wakes and the 'last rites'. The young girl has to rise above it all. Her duty is to know the voice of command that 'puts people in their places'.

So the amiable war hero and landowner, the girl's father, reckless in the saddle, will have a heart attack in mysterious circumstances; he is a charming drinker and accepted pursuer of young girls when he goes to London. When he is dying his freezing wife is indifferent; her role is to conserve the 'things' of the family – pictures, silver, fine inherited furniture, and the remains of the status and money. The role of the young girl is to control the war between wife, nurse, and the head-tossing servant who sneaks into the sickroom with fatal draughts of whiskey. She is the peasant with the pacifying art of giving sexual relief under the sheets: she pretends she is warming the old man's feet. What does the daughter crave? All the excitements of the freedom she has heard of in the Twenties: to be loved by the young man who has merely flirted in a gentlemanly way at a dance or two, and has vanished. She is red-faced, gauche, and clumsy in society, and has scarcely been educated by an ignorant governess hired mainly to teach her a few phrases of French as an item of gentility. What she craves is the assurance that her father is convinced of her virginity and that he loves *her*: he certainly hates his selfish wife. In the end he *does* show that he loves his daughter. He punishes his wife by leaving the girl the property. And the book ends with that great national festival, the classic Irish funeral at which the girl gets majestically drunk.

This book is an entertainment which in part recalls the one outstanding Irish novel of the nineteenth century, *The Real Charlotte* by E. O. Somerville and Martin Ross – the latter was the more sensitive and serious partner in the collaboration of Somerville and Ross in, for example, *Further Experiences of an Irish R.M.* Somerville was the mistress of country house farce and its metaphors ('Birds burst out of holly bushes like corks out of soda water bottles.' We remember old Flurry Knox whose 'grandmother's curry' was so powerful that 'you'd take a splint off a horse with it'.) Ross was the subtler social moralist who could almost match Mrs Gaskell's *Wives and Daughters* or, on native grounds, Maria Edgeworth.

Molly Keane's real novel, substantial and ingeniously organised, is the more recent *Time After Time*. It is more Ross than Somerville in temper than the earlier book. Now good behaviour is in abeyance, although its shadow is there. We are now in a period closer to the present day. Still no politics, though there is a horrified glance at a political crime abroad, the Holocaust.

For the rest, the Irish imbroglio tells its own tale. Elderly Jasper Swift and his three sisters look back on past glories as they quarrel in the Big House while its remaining acres have become a wilderness. The family are all old, the youngest in her sixties, the others in their late seventies. There are no comic servants, there is little money. Jasper, once at Eton, paces about in the patched clothes of his dressy youth: he has been left the terrible legacy of looking after his bickering and pitiless sisters. His realm is in the kitchen. He does the cooking, specialising in dubious menus with strange sauces which he recalls from his gourmet past; some of the stuff has been rescued from the dogs and cats and is made anonymous by a last-minute scattering of herbs. He is a quiet, nervy fellow and doesn't bother now to conceal his faintly homosexual past; a sort of half-fey cunning saint whose main relief – apart from cooking – is ruling his sisters by getting his own back. They are tough, high-spirited, unsexed ladies but bottled in illusions about their youth. In a confusing narrative which ingeniously brings back glimpses of the family past – and without any clumsy use of flashback so that the past secretes itself in fragments – we are grateful that the ladies are conveniently called April, May and June.

Fiercely they lock their bedrooms against one another. They have all, including Jasper, been emotionally maimed by the monstrous, possessive will of their 'darling Mummie', long ago dead. We are back in a forgotten Anglo–Irish, perhaps totally Irish, puzzle: how do the women survive? The answer is by secretiveness, rancour; liberated by isolation, they go 'underground' and 'make do', all expert in the 'home truth'.

Shut up in her room, seventy-five-year-old April, the ex-beauty, lives among the beautiful dresses of her past. She is a childless widow – she knows what the others don't, that 'thing men do'. (Her husband, a pornographer, liked 'doing it' on trains.) She lives in the past, and is deaf and carries a pad on which the others have to write down what they have to say. Her chief occupations are weight-watching and push-ups. Her deafness seems to enhance what was once beauty: she is 'armoured for loneliness'. She sips vodka and is bemused by tranquillisers.

May's room is as bleak as a room in a nursing-home. She looks and lives like a robot, has never been desired, but is frantically busy as a bad artist. She makes pictures out of tweed, grasses, dead flowers, and leather. She loves to collect china rabbits – her obsession. She is also light-fingered where bright little objects are concerned: tinsel, marbles, anything that shines – a jackdaw. Her dexterity with her hands is astonishing for she was born with a 'cropped right hand with only two fingers'. She knows how to conceal this wound at local talks on flower arrangement. She is in conspiracy also with the local antique dealer – a new type in modern Ireland – and is not above some skilful stealing.

Baby June, the youngest, aged sixty-four, has reverted to the peasant condition and is indeed a by-blow. Fit to do the work of two men, illiterate, she is a powerful girl in the stables and has been, in her time, a rider who was the terror of every point-to-point in the country and was 'the shape and weight of a retired flat race jockey'. She is an expert at delivering calves, killing lambs, knows how to deal with farrowing pigs. She clumps into the house, satisfied by the blood on her hands and clothes. Her closest friend and pupil is a pious Catholic stable-lad she

[61]

is training to become a jockey. Around the sisters crowd their lascivious dogs and cats in Jasper's filthy kitchen. (*His* cat sits on the bread board.)

And then, a pitiless figure descends on them – old indeed, fat but in gorgeous clothes, reeking of Paris and insinuation. She is Leda, half-Jewish, the daughter of a famous restaurateur in Vienna who had married into the family before the 1940 war. To her cousins she brings back the childhood memories of past wealth and pleasure. Miraculously they feel rejuvenated. They had never liked to talk about her because of her Jewish blood, for they were sure she had been trapped by the Nazis and had died in Belsen. They half-remember that, when staying with them as a girl, she had been suddenly, without explanation, and in one of the high moments of 'good behaviour' – 'so sorry you cannot stay' – firmly sent off at a moment's notice by 'darling Mummie', a genius of the final goodbye. Perhaps it was something to do with Daddy or Jasper? It doesn't matter now: they are ravished by her miraculous chatter. They are overcome by pity for her state: she is blind. Only Baby June, illiterate, dirty, has no time for her. Jasper himself, the man who had always longed to be a 'more of a Human Being', is excited. He returns to compete with Vienna in his kitchen. Leda, in short, brings the family to life. They put her in Mummie's sacred room and thenceforth she worms their secrets out of them. It is a seduction with a special compensation: her blindness. She cannot see how aged they all are, any more than she can know her own ugliness.

But when we see Leda installed alone in Mummie's sacred room we watch her do a strange thing. She gropes towards the wardrobe where Mummie's beautiful dresses still hang and, fingering the material, pulls the finest one out and spits all over it. Leda, we see, is here for vengeance. (Here is the real echo of the appalling jealousy Martin Ross evoked in *The Real Charlotte*.) One by one she worms out the eager secrets: April, full of erotic notions, picked up from her dead husband the pornographer; May the artist and nimble shoplifter; guilty Baby June who once shot Jasper in the eye when she was a child of seven; and Jasper, with his peculiar meetings with a local monk. At a terrible breakfast scene she comes out with all of it. Jasper in his lazy, evasive, semi-saintly way gladly makes himself out to be worse than the sisters who drive him mad, in order not to look nicer than they are.

There is more to this thoroughly well-organised traditional study of intrigue, malice, and roguery. It is rich and remarkable for the intertwining of portraits and events. It is spirited, without tears. The ingenious narrative is always on the move and has that extraordinary sinuous, athletic animation that one finds in Anglo–Irish prose. Mrs Keane has a delicate sense of landscape; she is robust about sinful human nature and the intrigues of the heart, a moralist well weathered in the realism and the evasions of Irish life. No Celtic twilight here! Detached as her comedy is, it is also deeply sympathetic and admiring of the stoicism, the *incurable* quality of her people. When Leda herself is exposed and is taken off and put back with her nuns again, a helpless, cynical, evil creature, April relentlessly goes with her, almost like a wardress, to make her do her slimming exercises. Jasper, who has never quite been able to become a 'human being', has one less sister to torment and turns once more to his cooking and gardening. So Irish realism, with the solace of its intrigues, dominates this very imaginative and laughing study of the anger that lies at the heart of the isolated and the old, and their will to live.

Le Roy Ladurie

MEDIEVAL VOICES

At the beginning of the fourteenth century, the Inquisition set out to crush the Albigensian, or Cathar, heresy in one of its last resorts, the tiny mountain village of Montaillou, on the French side of the Pyrenees, in what is now the Department of Ariège. In medieval times, the region was an independent principality ruled by the Comtes de Foix. A verbatim report of the proceedings of the Inquisition lies in the Vatican Library and had long been known to historians, who apparently regarded it as worthy of not much more than a footnote in their studies. History has traditionally been concerned with great persons and central political situations, but in recent years a number of French historians associated with the journal *Annales* have taken another view. They have turned from public life to the intimate and natural life of people caught as they live through events: to the daily habits, the superstitions and beliefs of anonymous men and women. The Inquisitor's report on Montaillou turned out, quite unintentionally, to be a mine rich with the everyday habits of an isolated group of peasants given idealistically to human error. Emmanuel Le Roy Ladurie, a fine and original historian – well known for his *The Peasants of Languedoc* – saw the peculiar value of the document, and although one might think an exhaustive study of Pyrenean peasant life in the fourteenth century to be outside the common interest, his *Montaillou: Cathars and Catholics in a French Village 1294–1324*, was a best-seller in France. The English translation, by Barbara Bray, is an abridgment of the French, but it is well done and irresistible.

   M. Le Roy Ladurie conveys his wide and searching scholarship in a graceful, clear, and witty prose. His intelligence sparkles. One reason for the book's success is overwhelming: the Inquisitor's verbatim report

[64]

enabled the author to give us what history so rarely can – the real voices and phraseology of a people lost for hundreds of years. We hear them talk of their village, crops, families, animals; their attitude to love, sex, marriage, death; their superstitions, their friends and enemies; their religious speculations. One is listening to an artless, sometimes sturdy, sometimes cunning confession. The whole might be the puzzled confession of a culture and an age. It was winkled out of them by the sly Inquisitor Jacques Fournier, Bishop of Pamiers, later Pope Benedict XII, who might almost be called the hostile co-author of Le Roy Ladurie's book. Fournier, we are told, was the 'very devil of an Inquisitor' – a remorseless psychologist and deadly theologian, a terrible sifter of souls. No detail of his victims' lives was too small for his attention. Had he not been a theologian, he might have been a novelist collecting his material. He also resembles the contemporary commissar, depending on spies and informers, and determined to destroy heterodox Error. Although Fournier was rarely a torturer, he had the sadistic pleasure of sending his victims to the stake or to be fettered in prison, where they were forgotten, and of sending the minor sinners to homeless ruin and the wearing of a yellow cross as a penalty for heresy.

It is not necessary for Le Roy Ladurie to go deeply into the Cathar heresy except in so far as it reveals the daily life of Montaillou, which became its last refuge; over the passes, the fugitives could get to the relative tolerance of Catalonia and the Mediterranean. The heresy was Christian and appeared originally in Languedoc, northern Italy, and the Balkans. In an eccentric form it foreshadowed the great Protestant revolt in Europe two centuries later. Catharism is evidence of a slowly growing change of heart and mind among the common people. It accepted the Manichaean doctrine of two opposite principles; one of good, one of evil – light and darkness, the spiritual and the carnal. God and Satan were equal or nearly equal gods. Cathar belief distinguished between believers, or *crédentes*, and an élite of personal righteousness the *parfaits*, or *bonshommes*. The *parfaits* were commonly said to be 'hereticated' – an equivalent of 'baptised'. They had to refuse to eat meat or to unite with women. Conversion assured them of immortality in a peasant Heaven; they were missionaries and could bless bread. Baptism was by book, not

[65]

by water. The cult was practised without Church ritual, in the privacy of the home. At death, the *parfaits* entered into a state of ascetic *endura*, or suicidal fasting. Less austere believers had a more agreeable life. They profited by one of the paradoxes of dualism: when everything is forbidden, everything becomes allowed (as the 'justified' sinners among Calvinists later discovered) until the last moments before death. Then ordinary believers might also become 'hereticated', and would be assured of the consolations of forgiveness and immortality – in which reincarnation played an ingenious part. The soul became part of a multitude of spirits that fill the air or enter animals:

> When the spirits come out of a fleshy tunic that is a dead body [said Belibaste, one of the villagers interrogated], they run very fast for they are fearful. They run so fast that if a spirit came out of a dead body in Valencia and had to go into another living body in the Comté de Foix, if it was raining hard, scarcely three drops of rain would touch it! Running like this, the terrified spirit hurls itself into the first hole it finds free! In other words into the womb of some animal which has just conceived an embryo not yet supplied with a soul; whether a bitch, a female rabbit or a mare. Or even in the womb of a woman.

Bad souls become devils, entering wolves, snakes, toads, flies, and all poisonous beasts, inedible or inimical to man.

The peasants were less hostile to religion than they were to increases in Church tithes, to the greed and worldliness of powerful priests, to taxes on humble foods such as cheese, beets, and turnips, to the rising price of Indulgences. Official Christianity became a political ideology. The peasants, weavers, and shepherds of a remote mountain village like Montaillou may have been in fee to the Comte de Foix, but the village was almost classless. The small castle that stood above the community, which hung down the mountainside, one house above another, had its châtelain, but the nobles were almost indistinguishable from the rest of the people. One of the most compelling women in this book is Béatrice de Planissoles, the châtelaine, who had had two 'noble' husbands and also several village lovers outside her caste. She could pass for a primitive village woman, as dirty in body as everyone else was, though not in hands and face, and, like the others, she would sit by the hearth delousing her husbands, her lovers, and the assembled family. Delousing was a common social way of passing time. Caste feeling was far slighter in the South of France than in the North, and in Montaillou poverty excluded it. The village had little dependence on the châtelain. The peasant did not feel inferior to the artisan, nor did the artisan feel inferior to the often ragged noble. The poverty was not wretched: the village lands were too cold for the vine, but there was wheat. The people lived on bread, smoked pork, the trout of the mountain streams, snails, and the squirrels in the forests. The familiar terraced plots of southern Europe grew enough. Money was scarcely used; barter replaced it. Domestic utensils being scarce, too, these were borrowed. To be free of temptation and spies, the *parfaits* lived a good deal in the forests, chopping timber, which the women carried home. There was a tailor who was a *parfait* and a cobbler who distinctly was not. It was a general rule in such villages that the cobblers and the priests were the Don Juans and contributed to the supply of bastards, who often became domestic servants. The rate of mortality was very high, especially among infants.

The moral centre of the society was the *ostal*, or *domus* – or, as we would say, the hearth. A family was not simply the persons in it but the stone, wood, or daub that housed them and their beasts, and the energies that sustained them. To protect these energies in the future, the hair and the fingernails of the corpse were preserved when the head of a family died; these were known to grow after death and were kept to stop the dead taking away the vitality of the *domus*. Another danger to the *domus* was the loss of women by marriage: they took their dowry with them. The villagers therefore negotiated marriages with the care of auditors making a balance sheet. Some, including the priest, inclined to the daydream of incest between brothers and sisters as a guarantee, but the defence of the family introduced subtler rules; marriage between first cousins was prohibited. Outside of this, Catharism was permissive without being promiscuous. There was a distinction between what was shameful and what was sin. Raymond de l'Aire, a peasant – and a confessed atheist – said:

To sleep with one's mother, sister or first cousin is not a sin, but it is shameful. On the other hand, to sleep with second cousins and other women I do not consider a sin, nor a shameful act either; and I hold firmly to this view, because in Sabarthès there is a proverb which says, 'With a second cousin, give her the works'.

The *parfaits* of Montaillou were revered as the 'goodmen', the bearers of virtue in a primitively Christian faith. But not all the inhabitants were heretics, and the Inquisition turned the place into a web of spies and informers. In Fournier's report, three or four figures come vividly to life. First, the brothers Clergue. Bernard was the tax collector and bailiff of the Comte de Foix. Pierre was the priest. He is the complex exemplar of the man who runs a protection racket – the godfather, or spider at the centre of a complex web. A short, frightening, blackmailing seducer of the women of his parish but a very able man, he was the son of a Cathar father, who detested him, and a Cathar mother, whom he adored. In his early years, he seemed to be a genuine heretic, but, intent on power, he soon became a double agent, and his brother co-operated with him. Bernard collected tithes and, to keep in with both sides, shared them between the Cathars and the orthodox Catholics. Neither brother saw himself as a renegade; rather, each saw himself as carrying out a justified vendetta against his family's enemies. Although the Clergues' evidence led many to be condemned, the Inquisition sent the brothers to death in prison when their dirty work was done.

Then, there is Béatrice de Planissoles. She would never consent to bear a child outside her own caste. She endured rape by the priest's cousin, a bastard, but does not seem to have been greatly distressed. Her love affairs were public; she was a sensual and passionate creature. Even the priest would not give her a child, for he recognised that he was lowborn and knew that she would be shamed. Yet he would sleep with her secretly, before the altar, on a bed brought into the church. He also practised a form of birth control, using a package of herbs containing the rennet of a hare.

One day, [said Béatrice,] I asked the priest: 'Leave your herb with me.'
'No,' he said, 'I won't, because then you could be united carnally

with another man, and thanks to the herb avoid becoming pregnant by him!'

The priest said that out of jealousy of Pathau, his cousin, who had been my lover before him.

Although the strength of the *domus* lay, as everyone knew, in marriage, the interrelationships often made marriage difficult. Concubinage was acceptable, and distinctions were made about the nature of love. The daughter of a sheep farmer formed a temporary union with Arnaud Vital, the cobbler. She said:

I was very fond of Arnaud, with whom I had established a dishonourable familiarity; he had instructed me in heresy; and I had promised him to go and see my mother to persuade her to agree that my young brother [he was very ill] should be hereticated.

Le Roy Ladurie notes that she did not think her life anything to hide or to be ashamed of – this was a real love affair, a matter of inclination. Arnaud remained on good terms with his mistress's mother. Many women thought carnal love no sin so long as one made love for pleasure. When pleasure ceased, it became sin. The Inquisitor unearthed the astonishing variety of influences, whether realistic, religious, or simply innocent, on human feeling. It was considered no sin to go with a prostitute so long as one paid: the payment absolved.

Le Roy Ladurie is not an anecdotalist. Every word spoken adds something to our knowledge of how the people lived and felt. He notes how the women married many years earlier than the men, who aged rapidly, so that if women had a hard life when they were young they survived much longer and came to formidable positions of power as mothers-in-law and grandmothers. He notes that the women were great gossips (dangerous in this period of religious persecutions) but that there was no educational difference between the sexes – neither had any education. Discrimination did not appear until parish schools were intro- duced: these schools were attended only by boys. The women liked firing off questions to one another about their relatives, about childbirth, and, always, about who was or who was not a heretic. It was not until the coming of a more bourgeois civilisation, with its concern for privacy, that this kind of watching, eavesdropping, and spying chatter decreased.

The most attractive human being among the enlightened families of the narrow *domus*-dominated village is Pierre Maury, the shepherd. The shepherds, who drove their flocks in the seasonal migrations across the Pyrenees into Catalonia, had the unsettled character of nomads. They were great bread eaters. They might stay in houses for a while or sleep in barns. They changed their masters often, preferred their freedom to money, rarely married, and scorned to accumulate goods. Pierre Maury was, it is true, once tricked into a marriage – which lasted three days – by a delinquent *parfait* whose mistress was pregnant. The *parfait* missionaries had a technique of preaching to the shepherds as they trudged on their journeys. Though Pierre Maury dabbled in heresy, he was soon bored and sly. He would lead the preacher up the steepest paths of the mountain, so that he was too short of breath to preach:

> But the shepherd and the goodmen used to stop for a pleasant, if not always very liturgical, snack on the journey: galantine of trout, meat, bread, wine and cheese. They had a Cathar good time, while the tentacles of the Inquisition had not yet extended to an altitude of 1,300 metres.

At one time, Pierre dared to rescue his sister from her husband, who was beating her. Pierre was a free man who did not bear malice for long. When ridiculed for being tricked by the *parfait* into the false marriage, he continued to be friends with the man who sponged on him:

> . . . this unrequited friendship was not only the result of individual magnanimity. It belonged to a general background of Occitan [i.e. Provençal] culture and artificial relationships in which total brotherhood between friends unlinked by blood, who shared everything equally without hesitation, was institutionalized in the ritual forms of fraternity (*affrèrement*), recorded from the beginning of the fourteenth century.

An informer called Sicre – a man as repellent as Pierre Clergue, the priest – pretended to enjoy Pierre Maury's popularity and friendship; Maury was imprisoned by the Inquisitor. Maury was a happy fatalist. He believed

[70]

in freedom, preferring a full network of human relations – casual women picked up in taverns – to a wife he could not, he said 'afford' (though he was often wealthy, in a haphazard way). He chose a life based on fate freely accepted. Le Roy Ladurie adds, 'is this not the very definition of Grace?' Pierre Maury had only one luxury – 'a pair of good shoes of Spanish leather' – and he was careless of arrest by the Inquisition, 'leading a life that was both passionate and passionately interesting'.

Montaillou was concerned, as the author says at the end of this absorbing book, with the physical warmth of the hearth and the promise of the Albigensian peasant Heaven 'one within the other'. Now the terraced plots of such villages, as one can see everywhere in the mountains of southern Europe, are being abandoned. The stability of an ancient world has gone. Our own world's new peasantry is in the factories, and, unlike the people of Montaillou, belongs to a society of competitors and consumers.

Lorca

THE DEATH OF LORCA

Thirty-seven years after the killing of the poet Federico García Lorca, whose fame had already spread far beyond Spain at the time of his death, it is still impossible to be absolutely certain of the accomplices in the crime and the exact motives for it. Even now, when Lorca's name is rehabilitated in Spain – owing to foreign opinion – and the act has been officially deplored because of the damage it did (and still does) to the image of Franco's 'National Cause', the blame is shifted from one group to another, without naming names. People who might have told much have died; some who could tell have grown old, memories have become vague or evasive. In Granada people waver between caution and fantasy. As in southern Ireland after the civil war of the Twenties, among those once close to the crimes committed there are embarrassment, the wish to forget, generalised talk of personal jealousies and 'uncontrollable elements' that 'come to the surface' in such times.

In Granada, where Lorca died, there was for example a 'Black Squad' of lawless killers who were given *carte blanche* by Valdes, the civil governor, to terrorise the city. They mainly butchered workers in the streets or dragged the wounded from the hospitals. The names of many of these monsters are well known: many died violently, one committed suicide, one still thrives as a timber merchant, another became, of all things, a university professor. When the Franco apologists speak nowadays of 'uncontrollable elements' they half hope we shall think Lorca fell to them. In fact it has been established that the arrest and shooting were very much a hysterical official affair and the work of 'respectable' people in the quarrelling groups who were important in Granada. The moderate CEDA blames the Falange, the Falange blames the CEDA or the Acción Popular, and the story becomes a triangle of factions and provincial personalities. In any case the Andalusians are spontaneous inventors of hearsay and love to dramatise it. They play up, as the Irish play up to Joyce scholars.

Ian Gibson is the latest foreign investigator to go into the mystery. The pioneer, of course, was Gerald Brenan (the Spanish scholar who lived in Andalusia most of his life) in his *Face of Spain*, published in the Fifties. Since then the French writer Claude Couffon, like Brenan, thought the murder might have been a reprisal for the death of Benavente. However, this suggestion came from a hysterical speech by the blood-thirsty Queipo de Llano, who was trying to excuse his blunder in giving the order: Benavente lived long after the civil war. Queipo de Llano may very well have believed the rumour and it seems probable – and is indeed reported – that he told the hesitant governor of Granada to 'give him [Lorca] coffee, plenty of coffee' – Queipo's favourite euphemism when ordering an execution. Enzo Cobelli, an Italian, came to the conclusion that Lorca was a pawn in the struggle between the Falange and the Army represented by a Captain Nestares, who was in charge of the executions at Viznar. (Nestares is still alive, very rich, but Mr Gibson could get nothing out of him.)

A third work, by Marcelle Auclair, seems to Mr Gibson to come closer to probability. It is well established that an informer or agent called Ruiz Alonso played a part in the arrest of Lorca, who was hiding in the house of a close Falangist friend, Rosales. The Rosales family were political enemies of Ruiz Alonso, who was a religious fanatic, and he decided to get them into trouble for hiding the poet. A fourth work, by Jean-Louis Schonberg, argued that there was nothing political in the arrest and that it was a vengeance springing out of homosexual jealousy. (Lorca was indeed homosexual, though he regarded himself as one of the 'pure' as distinct from the 'impure' homosexuals.) In Schonberg's argument Ruiz Alonso was also homosexual and was jealous of the poet. This was exploited by a Granadino painter, in order to save his own skin. (When Gibson put this to Ruiz Alonso he made a dramatic rhetorical scene, proclaimed his heterosexual virility was famous, and offered to seduce the women folk of the critics who denied it.) I agree that Schonberg sounds like an erotic sensationalist taking advantage of the myth of Spanish *machismo*.

Mr Gibson's patient examination of the known evidence and his own further, persistent inquiries, which include interviews that were very bold, have led him to believe that the persecution of Lorca was initiated:

> ... not by any one man but by a group of ultra-Catholic and like-minded members of Acción Popular, among whom Ramón Ruiz Alonso, as an ex-deputy of the CEDA, was the most influential.

The men who took Lorca off from the Rosales house with Ruiz Alonso included a rich landowner called Trecastro and one other. All were members of that fanatical religious group. All, except Alonso, are dead. Trecastro, a roystering Andalusian womaniser and therefore a hero of the Granada cafés, boasted of his part in the arrest and, seemingly, the execution. These things do not constitute proof but there is no doubt that the Acción Popular hated Lorca for his family contacts with the liberal intellectuals of Granada who had brought a celebrity to the city which is now lost and sold to package tourism.

The labyrinth to which this book introduces us is incomprehensible without knowledge of Spanish history, the conflict of the intellectuals with the Church in the nineteenth and twentieth centuries, and the politics of the Second Republic after 1931. Fortunately Mr Gibson is succinct about these matters and is particularly good on the situation in Granada. The picturesque and moribund city had become attractive to distinguished foreigners and Spaniards, and a centre for artists and intellectuals drawn first by the beauty of the Alhambra, which was being intelligently restored, and by Adalusian music. By the end of the century the university had an enormously influential figure in the person of the socialist Fernando de los Ríos, whose family were closely connected with the brilliant anti-clerical educationalists and writers known as 'the generation of '98'. They have had no successors.

At the same time, the city had become rich by the introduction of the sugar beet into the fertile *vega* outside it; a new, wealthy bourgeoisie grew up and *their* Granada, already deep in the fame of being a symbol of the defeat of the Moors, the persecution of the Jews, and the unification of the country, was now about the most obdurately conservative city of the south and beginning to feel the world-wide economic depression. Conditions of life for the peasants were bad; they had begun to organise themselves politically; the middle classes were undoubtedly terrified. It is interesting that Ruiz Alonso – not a native of the province – came from a family that had gone downhill; he had become a printer. His resentment was the classic fascist one of the lower-middle-class 'chip'. The established rich in Spain have always held to the traditionalist Catholicism and the militant and violently intolerant spirit of the Counter-Reformation. From the early nineteenth century onward they have been totally opposed to liberal reform, especially in education.

By the Twenties – when I first went to Granada and spent some time with Fernando de los Ríos – I was, like most foreigners, astonished by the absolute division between the Catholic and the liberal groups. There was not merely hostility of opinion, there were personal hatred, social ostracism, and undeclared civil war. The hatred was for the intellect, especially for an intellect which had contacts outside Spain. The Acción Popular would hate Lorca simply because he was a playwright and poet, famous everywhere and connected with the intelligentsia in Granada, Madrid, Paris, and New York. Politically he was naïve: he was simply and generously on the side of the poor, for his art derived from the popular culture of the *vega*. But he had no party connections; for him 'the people' did not mean 'the People' of left-wing politicians. He was closely related to the de los Ríos family, but he was equally a friend of the Falangist Rosales and of the young José Antonio Primo de Rivera, leader of the Falange.

To Lorca, as to hundreds of gifted and independent people like him, the anarchic state of Spain was a torment that frightened him. It was in deep depression and fear that he went home to his family in Granada when the rising was about to break. It seems that Ruiz Alonso was on the night train that took Lorca to Granada. When, weeks later, Alonso came to the house of Rosales where Lorca was hiding and Rosales asked what charges were made against the poet, Alonso's reply was, 'He did more damage with his pen than others with their guns.' In that there is all the rancour of the slave turned informer.

One of Mr Gibson's achievements is to have secretly taped Alonso's rambling rhetorical attempts in old age to blow up his importance and disown his responsibility. There are streams of religious justification and self-praise. If in the end Mr Gibson's indefatigable inquiries bring no certainty, they have led him through the ghastly scenes of the Franco terror in Granada. Over 4000 people were shot in the city alone. The trucks loaded up the prisoners, among them a large number of famous lawyers, doctors, surgeons, university professors, and carried them out night after night to be shot against a country wall.

Readers of this book may think of it as an exercise in detection, and a very able one, and may be tempted to say, with the Franco sympathisers, that the same went on on both sides. It did. But as Mr Gibson says:

> Had Federico not died that morning at Víznar, the thousands of other innocent, but less well known, *granadinos* liquidated by the rebels might have been forgotten. As it is they will be remembered long after those responsible for the repression have passed into oblivion.

Seen in this light of course Lorca's death has a symbolic significance that goes far beyond Granada to the thousands who fell to the ferocity which Franco awakened in a nation notoriously prone to it.

André Malraux

MALRAUX AND PICASSO

———

In his essays on painting and sculpture André Malraux was a master of eloquence and aphorism. He had been a Marxist, drawn romantically to revolutions – first in the Far East and then, as a soldier, in the Spanish Civil War. He was also, mysteriously, a collector and an entrepreneur, and, finally, a Minister of Cultural Affairs whose hero was de Gaulle. Malraux was deeply a hero-worshipper. His famous novels were laconic. Later, flights of pugnacious rhetoric came to illuminate his polemical writing like flashes of lightning, by which his subjects jumped into silhouette out of what one can only call a landscape of generalisations. This quality dominates *Picasso's Mask*, the essay he wrote in the last year of his life. The book is a moving and pointed recollection of talks about painting that he had with Picasso over the years. It is also a fighting commentary on the 'Copernican revolution' that changed the direction of Western painting and sculpture after 1900, when the West made its contacts with Asian, African, and prehistoric art. Added to this, there is a very personal campaign for what he calls the Museum Without Walls, in which certain works of genius can look across the centuries and, as he puts it, 'whisper' to one another. Such a museum, it is agreed, must ideally exist in the mind; artists, in any case, fear museums. Malraux's first flash of lightning makes this distinction:

What did the Louvre assert? What was Giotto's response to Cimabue and to the Byzantine mosaics of the baptistry in Florence, which he passed each day? Art is an interpretation of nature – of what men can see . . .

In many respects the Renaissance was a resurrection of the visible.

[77]

In many respects, the Museum Without Walls is a resurrection of the invisible.

In a famous phrase – an echo of Dostoevski's 'Without art a man might not find his life worth living' – art, for Malraux, is 'a revolt against man's fate'. It is 'a manifestation of what men are unable to see: the sacred, the supernatural, the unreal . . .'

Picasso, parodist, destroyer and creator, the most prolific inventor of styles and forms, was exactly the figure to attract Malraux's electricity. Of the private Picasso he says little, though what he does say is touching and vivid: we see Malraux after his escape from Spain in the Civil War talking to the painter while he is working on 'Guernica'; we see them again in the studio in the Rue des Grands-Augustins, and still later in Provence. There is little about politics. After Picasso died, Malraux went down to the farmhouse, Notre-Dame-de-Vie, at Mougins, in which each room was the painter's workshop and where one walked as on a jungle path through canvases stacked everywhere. He was called in to help the grieving Jacqueline Picasso – the pretty girl from Arles, 'a Roman medal with an aquiline nose' – in her difficulties about housing the painter's work and collection. Appropriately near to Mougins, the first experimental embodiment of a Museum Without Walls, which he and Picasso had often discussed, was opened in 1973, at the Fondation Maeght. There, in 'secret confabulation' across time, were the pieces of Asian statuary, the 'Penelope' looted from the Acropolis, the 'Kacyapa' of Lung-Men, Manet's 'Berthe Morisot', the Beauvais 'King', Rouault's 'Worker's Apprentice', some Fauves, and, of course Braques and Picassos, and much else. Missing were Courbet's 'Portrait of Baudelaire' – one of Malraux's 'saints' – and there was no Monet. Picasso had no Realists or Impressionists in his personal collection. For Picasso, 'the saints acting as intercessors' were Cézanne, Van Gogh, and Douanier Rousseau.

The word 'intercessors' is arresting. When Picasso was painting 'Guernica', he spoke of the influence of Japanese painting on his immediate predecessors, and of his own encounter with Negro sculpture:

The [Negro] masks weren't just like any other pieces of sculpture. Not at all. They were magic things. But why weren't the Egyptian pieces or the Chaldean? . . . Those were primitives, not magic things. The Negro pieces were *intercesseurs*, mediators . . . They were against everything – against unknown, threatening spirits. I always looked at fetishes. I understood; I too am against everything. I too believe that everything is unknown, that everything is an enemy! Everything! Not the details – women, children, babies, tobacco, playing – but the whole of it! . . . all the fetishes were used for the same thing. They were weapons. To help people avoid coming under the influence of spirits again, to help them become independent. They're tools. If we give spirits a form, we become independent. Spirits, the unconscious (people still weren't talking about that very much), emotion – they're all the same thing. I understood why I was a painter.

And this led him on to the disputes with Braque: Braque wasn't afraid of the masks, didn't even find them foreign to him; he had not a trace of superstition. Also Braque *reflected* when he worked. Picasso put curiosity before reflection:

Personally, when I want to prepare for a painting, I need things, people. He's lucky: he never knew what curiosity was . . . He doesn't know a thing about life; he never felt like doing everything with everything.

The pair had, said Jacqueline, awful rows. Picasso hated continuity of style; his successive periods follow one another 'like outbursts within rage'.

He grumbled: 'Down with style! Does God have a style? He made the guitar, the Harlequin, the dachshund, the cat, the owl, the dove. Like me. The elephant and the whale – fine – but the elephant and the squirrel? A real hodgepodge! He made what doesn't exist. So did I. He even made paint. So did I.'

Picasso's condemnation of style, Malraux says, was more profound and also more obscure than his remark 'I have no real friends. I have only lovers! Except perhaps for Goya, and especially Van Gogh.' In later life, he would have added Rembrandt. What a painter has to do, Picasso argued, was to revolutionise people's way of identifying things – create images they wouldn't accept, a world that was not reassuring. He liked to think of himself as a 'sorcerer' (and some have thought of his works as acts of exorcism); Malraux notes that the word 'was in keeping with the trancelike states of some of his forms'. His figures come out of 'black magic, his power of metamorphosis'. Picasso knew that 'his genius had a mysterious side to it; he was aware of his malarial fits of invention'. He had, Braque said, a sleepwalking side. Of course, if one is conscious of violence and anarchy – which strike me as having deep roots in the Spanish tradition – there is also something of the child's free imagination, inventiveness, and feeling for play, the child's impatience. One day, Malraux recalls, Picasso took out of a metal cupboard a violin-shaped idol from the Cyclades and two casts of a prehistoric statuette – the Lespugue Venus. One was of the mutilated statuette. The other was of the statuette restored: '. . . her bust, and her legs joined together, sprang forth symmetrically from the lusty volume of her rump and her belly.' A grotesque? No. A new object buzzing with its new life. Picasso said, darkly, 'I could make her by taking a tomato and piercing it through with a spindle, right?' He sounded, Malraux says in another connection, as if he were poking fun at himself, though often he seemed to be jeering at the human form: 'His jokes were grating.'

This essay is not the work of an art historian, or even of a critic, but, rather, the rhetorical response of a man of action to some of the artist's innumerable acts with his hands. (Like others of his generation, Picasso rejected the word 'artist'. He hated 'professionalism'. The professionals were just turning out cakes and confectionery of the required kind. Aesthetics were an irrelevance.) To Malraux, who had a lot of the old Marxist left in him, evaluation and the question of beauty are matters of history, and history has now become much wider in our own minds. How does he relate Picasso, the genius of metamorphosis, to our need for art, and how do we know our standards? How is it that we can tell the difference, say, between Surrealism and Picasso's fantastic invention, between the *tableau vivant* and folk invention, between accident and design? These are questions of value that writers have put to painters hotly since the 'Copernican revolution' – questions notoriously futile from the painter's point of view. Painting and sculpture cannot be translated into words. One art cannot evoke another.

[80]

We have to turn to the very long and sweeping speech that Malraux made when his idea of a Museum Without Walls was modestly realised at the Fondation. The address is the brilliant glissade of a mind through the sacred and profane phases of Western art from pre-Christian times to the paganism of today. His aphorisms and paradoxes cut like forked lightning. One has to be quick to see the silhouettes of artistic crises as they jump out and pass. His mind is combative. To those who may be thinking of Spengler, the decline of the West, and that all is chaos, Malraux replies that 'the Museum Without Walls is based on the assumption that the destiny of all great styles is metamorphosis'.

> Artists had represented the characters of Classical mythology in accord-ance with faith, but they then came to represent the characters of the Christian faith in accordance with Classical mythology.

With Romanticism, the whole world of art changed: 'The glory of the word "beauty" came to an end with Delacroix.' The painters no longer said, 'It's beautiful'; they said, 'It's good.' Realism, for Malraux, derives from the idealism and spiritualism of the Romanticism that preceded it, and against which it fights. Manet's 'Olympia' did away with 'the illusion and the poem' in Titian's 'Venus of Urbino', and is a reincarnation. The power to create may originate, as we know well,

> from the most disquieting unpredictability, from a madman's inspi-ration, from the naïveté of the naïve, or from the patience of a shepherd . . .

but it 'harmonises its own elements in a way that life never does'. All historical civilisations have carried on 'a dialogue with the unknowable', and the unknowable 'encompasses death, sacrifice, cruelty . . .'; it is 'a mixture of what man hopes to know and what he will never know'. Finally:

> Our civilization, which now sees that of the nineteenth century as a hesitant and optimistic preface to it, is not devaluing its awareness of the unknowable; nor is it deifying it. It is the first civilization that has severed itself from religion and superstition. In order to question it.

And the forms of our art 'have become as arbitrary as the forms of the sacred . . .'.

What would Picasso, the painter who worked all day and half the night, sometimes in a fever, sometimes humorously and ingeniously at play – what would he have made of this speech? I think he would have been struck by precise instances rather than by argument. From what Malraux says in an aside earlier in the book, both he and Picasso seem to have been astonished that a form like the stained-glass window, 'which awoke and fell asleep in accordance with the passing of day', was forsaken. It gave in and died when painting turned to the discovery and innovation of shadow. Five hundred years passed before painters rediscovered 'the arbitrary element' in the stained-glass window, and in mosaics. Whimsically, but with dire meaning, Malraux adds, 'When stained-glass windows vanished, clocks began to reign over the churches.' The epigram allows a laugh of pleasure to the reader of a strenuous book that rather overpowers the subject. (Malraux was equally overpowering in his well-known essay on Goya.) Malraux engages us most when he digs up the dear old rows about art which kept Paris alive until, after the last war, they moved on to New York.

Thomas Mann

THE ROMANTIC AGONY

Thomas Mann was one of those formidable novelists who strike us as being men of iron, locked in ambition, eloquent on the podium, cold in detachment, and brimming with erudition. He is the high-bourgeois artist who claims the rights of the artist-prince yet nevertheless looks down with the melancholy of the artist-surgeon seeking intimations of our mortality. There are glints of a romantic sadism in that gaze, which has come to be thought of as a characteristic of 'the Romantic Agony' common in his generation. He himself knew that this tormented spirit was penetrated by the strong influence of the Protestant work ethic, which he inherited from his mercantile forebears, who had been eminent in Lübeck for generations. He can indeed be thought one of the great martyrs of that ethic, but it is untrue to add, as some critics have, that 'he starved his life to feed his art'. In an Afterword to the biographical study *Thomas Mann: The Making of an Artist 1875–1911*, by Richard Winston, the biographer's widow writes that Thomas Mann was 'bewilderingly caught up in life'. 'He had fought with great energy on literary and political battlefields. Several times over he had seen the stable world around him crashing to pieces. He had had more than his share of acquaintances, alliances, loves, hates, tragedies. In fact, Mann's personal history had all the elements of a great novel.' Alas, Mr Winston died in 1979, halfway through that 'novel'. But he did reach the period of *Death in Venice* and was already aware of the sources of the masterpieces of old age, *Joseph and His Brothers* and *Dr Faustus*. Winston's book establishes 'the making', and, if it is rather crowded in detail, it is persuasive in its good sense and free from jargon – as indeed Mann himself was – and is fascinating as a human portrait and a literary enquiry. Mr Winston had translated some of the works and letters, had read Mann's very private diaries, and is always persuasive in his conclusions.

About Mann's famous 'cold' detachment: the accusation of coldness stung him. In 'Der Bajazzo' ('The Dilettante'), an early story, he wrote, 'It almost seems, does it not, that the quieter and more detached a man's outward life is, the more fierce and exhausting are his inward struggles.' But, as Mr Winson says, those early lines about himself turn halfway into a story about his elder brother, Heinrich, with whom Thomas's life was so entangled in their early years. They aimed their books at each other. The two young men united in their rebellion against the family – Heinrich the dashing leader at first, Thomas the more jealous in the bond. They were obsessed with each other even in their long quarrel in middle age. Heinrich was to pass from the dilettantism of the neo-Romantic into something closer to the social revolutionary. Thomas's own conservatism would eventually soften. If the Dilettante is Heinrich, the delightful childhood scenes in 'Der Bajazzo' are Thomas's. As for intellect, Thomas is at first the backward schoolboy, idle and dreamy; like Tolstoy, almost an autodidact. He is intoxicated by the myths and erotic sensations aroused by Wagner's operas, by Nietzsche's superman. As for the gloom of Schopenhauer, who captivated so many nineteenth-century novelists, Thomas was no philosopher yet believed that '. . . the will to live perpetually seeks to cancel out the results of its own blind strivings . . .'. For both youths, this was evident in their distinguished family's history: their wealthy father closed down his business in the Baltic grain trade when it showed signs of decline before the influences of the new 'imperialist capitalism'. The moral was that the belief in Will and the work ethic had created a longing for rest, for nirvana and death – a theme to become strong in Thomas, though taking a different direction in Heinrich. The message of Thomas's superb *Buddenbrooks*, written in his twenties, was not shirtsleeves to shirtsleeves in three generations but shirtsleeves to decadence and art.

The artistic impulse seems also to have had sources outside the North German tradition. The mother of the boys was solidly German, but she had been brought up in Brazil by a Portuguese mother; Mr Winston speaks of her as a kind of Latin mermaid who beguiled with her taste for music. Thomas was vain of this exotic foreign strain – talk of inherited 'blood' was a nineteenth-century obsession; also he was eager to call himself a 'philo-Semite', because he was strongly drawn to the cultivated Jewish circles in Lübeck, and in fact eventually married a rich, beautiful, intellectual Jewess.

Add these influences together, impose the torrential influences of Wagner's operas, and we have an imaginative artist who was his mother's son and an inveterate, if melancholy, disciple of the father's gospel of work. He said of himself in one of his intensely explicative essays, 'as a guardian of myth the writer is conservative. But psychology is the keenest sapper's tool known to democratic enlightenment.' He was certainly a master of irony and a mediator. One has to be wary of Mann's Flaubertian comments on art. There is always a mocking spirit in them. The most committed of artists, he saw the artist almost as a harlequin or a not-to-be-disturbed wanton – a man who turned from real life to 'puppets'. He wrote that he had no desire to deny or betray his vocation, but he held that fiction could be a serene, even sacred game, yet still a game. His erudition itself, he said, was a game or a feat of opportunism. He just 'worked things up':

> ... that is to collect information in order to play literary games with it – or strictly speaking, to scandalously misuse it. Thus I became in turn an expert in medicine and biology, a firm Orientalist, Egyptologist, mythologist and historian of religions, a specialist in medieval culture and poetry, and so on ... I forget with incredible speed everything I have learned.

Death in Venice is most delicate and exact as it catches the literal pleasure evoked by Venice and the Lido, but he carefully researched the cholera and the sinister Eastern winds that brought the plague to stagnate there; he researched the city's official policies in hushing up the rumours of the plague. In *Buddenbrooks*, he documented the rise and fall of the Baltic grain trade, the changes in real-estate values, the role of married women in sustaining the bourgeois ethos of the merchants, and their weariness of the cult of achievement. Not only did he document as required but, as many other artists have more accidentally done, he stored up passing experiences for use in the far future. When Thomas and his brother were in Italy as young men, they saw the famous Roman *Mosaico del Nilo*, with its fantastic crowd of elephants and crocodiles, in the medieval city of Palestrina; the experience came back to his mind in old age when he was reconstructing the anthropological myth that gives powerful meaning to *Joseph and His Brothers*. Documentation was not fact fetishism, as it was so often in the novels of Zola; it was not an aspect of Balzac's speculative greed. Facts turned into the myth that lifts one out of reporting and journalism into the images of art by which we live.

Yet if Thomas liked to think he had inherited a Latin strain through his mother, he was inescapably the prudent North German. He was both a Naturalist and a mythmaker: an ear man, he said, rather than an eye man. The brotherly rivalry came to a head when Heinrich wrote his extravagant novel *Die Göttinnen* as a fashionable erotic counterpart to *Buddenbrooks*. Thomas was appalled by Heinrich's paganism, and by the reckless prose and syntax, which he called bombast. When they were entranced by Italy, Heinrich felt at home there, Thomas was soon bored. Thomas was distinctly his own psychoanalyst: the affectionate sensuality, the conscienceless comedy of Neapolitan life, drove his young Northern mind inward. His sexuality froze. He wrote in his diary:

What am I suffering from? From knowledge – is it going to destroy me? What am I suffering from? From sexuality – is it going to destroy me? – How I hate it, this knowledge which forces even art to join it! How I hate it, this sensuality, which claims that everything fine and good is its consequence and effect. Alas, it is the *poison* that lurks in everything fine and good! – How am I to free myself of knowledge? By religion? – How am I to free myself of sexuality? By eating rice?

Yes; at least rice was cheap, and he had little money. Get back to the desk and work to drive away temptation. In Naples, he wrote a glum monologue called 'Disillusionment', which no one – except a curious biographer like Mr Winston – need read now. Yet – and this is Mr Winston's point – there was rarely any grist lost to Thomas Mann's mill.

[86]

He would wait forty years until the pimps who had tormented him in Naples were ready to be used in *Death in Venice*.

This brings us to what Mann called his secret homoeroticism, which came to light in the diaries published after his death, and which – to the happily married man – seemed a 'defect' in his nature. In his boyhood, he had passionately loved one or two of his school friends and in later life he had strongly erotic but entirely innocent attachments to young men. These attachments were, he said, a secret source of pleasure, interest, and creative power – the last, we must suppose, their most important aspect. Mr Winston thinks that Mann may have exaggerated the importance of the 'defect' as he exaggerated his headaches, his colds, his neurasthenia, his exhaustion, and that longing for nirvana, sleep, even death which derives from an excess of work and will. And Mr Winston notes that the attraction of young men or boys, or what Mann called *Knabenliebe*, was generally acceptable as a sort of education in the years of the Weimar Republic, and turned quickly to a greater attraction to women: the diagnostician was very familiar with Freud on the erotic spell of the mother–son relationship. *Death in Venice* derives from Mann's sense of his personal 'defect' and, such was public opinion at the time, the story caused a scandal when it was published. But stories rarely if ever spring from a single impulse. A work of art is a tranposition, even an evasion: real life, as it is, is no good. *Death in Venice* is a masterpiece not only because of its exact evocation of the scene but also because the writer drew on a variety of sources. Mann said that the book started in his head as a story based on the aged Goethe's disastrous passion for a very young girl, hardly more than a child. If Aschenbach in Venice is a tired old writer, he is neither Goethe nor Mann; he is even given the strange head of Mahler, the composer. The only intimate links with Mann are the Socratic dialogue from the Phaedrus (which Mann reread) and the use of obscene nightmare – a truly Wagnerian saturnalia that enabled him to make the carnal insinuation clear but blameless. Still, Mann *was* the perpetual autobiographer simply because he was not writing literal autobiography. Years later, a middle-aged Polish gentleman, living in Warsaw, wrote to Mann's daughter enclosing photographs of a boyhood holiday on the Lido. He claimed that he had been the original of the charming boy in *Death in Venice*. There he was, again and again, in the very clothes Mann had described. There stood his Polish mother and her family. Even the scrimmage on the beach had occurred. He said he remembered that there was a peculiar, puzzling old man who kept staring at him and following him about. The Warsaw gentleman was delighted to be so immortalised in a masterpiece.

Both Heinrich and Thomas, but especially the latter, were ruthless in their portraits of their families and intimates, exposing the secrets of those close to them, and, Mr Winston says, there is sometimes a suggestion of cruelty in this. Most novelists find that a character does not come to life until blended with others or altered by context. Mann's defence was very different:

> I should like to point out the error inherent in making a literal identification between reality and its artistic image. I should like to have a work of art regarded as something absolute, not subject to everyday questions of right and wrong.

Goethe, he said, had not insulted the real people portrayed in his *Werther*: On the contrary, Lotte and her husband

> ... realized that it would have been petty to hold a grudge against the writer who in his book had conferred upon them a life a thousand times superior, more intense and lasting than they were leading in their ordinary respectable reality – and they held their peace.

And, he added, if a portrait was hostile in any respect, the author was inevitably self-portrayed and attacking himself with the same detachment. We might add to this the self-irony in the reflections of Aschenbach, as Eros drives him to his desk:

> Verily it is well for the world that it sees only the beauty of the completed work and not its origins nor the conditions whence it sprang; since knowledge of the artist's inspiration might often but confuse and alarm and so prevent the full effect of its excellence. Strange hours, indeed these were, and strangely unnerving the labour that filled them.

[88]

Such hours, sometimes mundane and crowded with the agitations of German life of the period, have been skilfully sought in Mr Winston's biography. The disaster of the 1914 war, the rise of Hitler, Mann's flight from Germany, were yet to come, and Winston did not live to show Mann embattled.

V. S. Naipaul

IRAN AND PAKISTAN

In 1979 and '80 V. S. Naipaul travelled through Iran, Pakistan, Malaysia and Indonesia, in an attempt to get into the minds of students, villagers, traders, teachers and missionaries who had been swept emotionally into the Islamic revival. Some of the young students had been at British or American colleges and they particularly were convinced of the 'sickness' of the West – no religious faith – and of the evils of Western 'materialism'. Most had put their faith in the literal guidance in the primitive oracular work, the Koran, and its minute system of rewards and punishments and were preaching revolt by regress; others were revolutionary Marxists, above all in Teheran. We are faced in Iran by scenes of savagery, faction and ruin; underlying this is the belief that the Muslim faith contains the secret of spiritual 'wholeness' which the West has lost. At the same time, all are eager for the skills and, above all, the rewards of Western science and technology. In this confusion the mind is split. As Mr Naipaul goes eastward he is among peoples who are racially divided and they feel themselves to be lost and 'displaced'. When Muslims spoke to him of this he reminded them that he was a native of Trinidad whose family traditions were those of displaced Hindus, now without faith, and that the Western ethos had equipped him with the will to strive intellectually.

Mr Naipaul is a remarkable diagnostician and, above all, a fertile novelist. These gifts are the making of him as an admirable, thinking traveller who exposes himself to the scene. He is a born narrator in the small or large scene. Every place and person and mind comes to life. Like most travellers he uses all his wits to make people talk of themselves and he is so persistent in this that, again and again, it strikes us that they would not have known how to do so without his ingenious Socratic questioning. He is not out for 'copy' but to explore states of experience and mind. He is fully tutored in religious and secular history. He knows the Islamic past. He understands, for example, why the upheaval in Iran (up to now, in many respects, a civilised society) was possible because of its distance from the desert tradition. But, although sharp and decisive, he has a temperamental sympathy and even tenderness for his often intractable people.

Naipaul is far from being a fundamentalist. The Muslim fundamentalist, he notes, seeks to work back to a whole 'with the tool of faith alone – belief, religious practices and rituals. It is like a wish – with intellect suppressed or limited, the historical sense falsified – to work back from the abstract to the concrete, and to set up the tribal walls again.'

But he knows the Muslim mind is split and even idle:

The West, or the universal civilization it leads, is emotionally rejected. It undermines; it threatens. But at the same time it is needed, for its machines, goods, medicines, warplanes, the remittances from the emigrants, the hospitals that might have a cure for calcium deficiency, the universities that will provide master's degrees in mass media. All the rejection of the West is contained within the assumption that there will always exist out there a living, creative civilization, oddly neutral, open to all to appeal to. Rejection, therefore, is not absolute rejection. It is also, for the community as a whole, a way of ceasing to strive intellectually. It is to be parasitic; parasitism is one of the unacknowledged fruits of fundamentalism.

In the empty Hilton in ruined Teheran no sermons were too long for the idle desk clerk. Having got rid of the Shah the people believed that 'oneness was all that was still needed . . .'.

What, after the centuries of despotism, they really believed was that the state was something apart, something that looked after itself and was ever restored. And even while with their faith they were still pulling it all down – a hotel, city, state – they were waiting for it to start up again, to be as it was before.

[91]

His first interpreter in Teheran was a young science student, Behzad. He was not religious. He was a Communist, the son of a Communist father who had been imprisoned in the Shah's time and had inherited his father's dream of social justice. Behzad kept away from Mosques and the observances and was forcing himself to see in Khomeini's religious fervour the outline of the social revolution he wanted. For him the Ayatollah was a *petit bourgeois*. Behzad was a tormented young man because the revolution, except in its proletarian aspect, was not his: his hero was Stalin! He was compassionate and had the old Persian delicacy, but he hated Revolutionary Guards and mullahs. He warned Naipaul never to describe himself as having no religion. In the holy, learned and therefore dangerous city of Qom, Behzad took him to see the Ayatollah Shirazi, a benign teacher in the theological college. It had 14,000 students who would remain there for anything from six to fifteen or twenty years: 'as in medieval Europe, there was no end to theological scholarship'. Thinking had been reduced to the repetitious. One of the lecturers had produced material for a twenty-five-volume commentary on the Shia idea of the Imam. (The Ayatollah Khomeini, known for his studies in jurisprudence and Islamic philosophy, had also produced eighteen volumes on other topics!) Shirazi's accent was more Arabic than Persian as he intoned his conversation. And then came the crucial question 'What is *your* religion?' There were Pakistan students present and Naipaul felt he had to be wary before them: his own forebears were Hindus. Behzad told him to say he was Christian. Shirazi asked, 'But what kind of Christian?' Luckily Naipaul said, 'Protestant.' This half pleased the Ayatollah Shirazi who said, 'Then you are closer to the truth. Catholics are inflexible'; but as Naipaul acutely notes he was merely giving a Shia twist to Christian divisions. The Persians are Shias; with their heretical line of succession to the Prophet they see themselves as 'an embattled minority'. This, combined with the industrial wealth of the Shah's dispensation, gave the startling Persian revolution its hysteria and fanaticism: they saw themselves as the true heirs of the Faith. It struck me, twenty years ago when I was in Iran, that a pride in primitive tribal violence was just under the skin, even of the Westernised; and that it was blatant among the poor in the countryside.

At Qom Naipaul thought he had no chance of seeing the notorious hanging judge Khalkhalli but the message came back that the judge 'would *love* to see you'. The famous slaughterer was merely five feet tall, a quick-stepping little clown of a man with merry eyes and wearing glasses, crumpled clothes and a couple of cotton garments hanging over his slack white trousers. He boasted that he had started life as a shepherd – 'right now I know how to cut off a sheep's head' – and added that he had sentenced and killed the Shah's Prime Minister, Hoveyda. This was a joke, put on to make the crowd in his room roll with laughter.

'You killed him yourself?' the author asked, through his interpreter. (In fact Hoveyda had been killed by the son of an ayatollah.)

'But I have the gun,' the judge said. He said he had it in the next room: a treasure.

Foreign interviewers, as Naipaul says, are easy money; he knew the judge was a comedian and was using him as a straight man. He and Behzad returned to Teheran. There the student was to hear that the Left-Wing paper he worked for had been closed down; by the end of the book this earnest worshipper of Stalin finds his political group defeated for the moment: many of his friends are in prison, many are dead. 'We have to kill *all* the bourgeoisie. All the bourgeoisie of the oppressor class,' he said (with a sweet smile) as Naipaul left him to his mathematical work – done in his fine Persian script, with Western (or Arabic or Indian) numerals. Many of his textbooks were American. Behzad had been fed by so many cultures, Naipaul reflects, but now, at what should have been the beginnings of his intellectual life – like the Muslims to whom he was opposed – he had cut himself off.

In Iran one felt that money, foreign goods and tools, gave the illusions of Islamic power, for unearned dollars kept an idle country and its revolution 'on the boil'. In much poorer Pakistan, the tensions of poverty and political distress were falsified by crude rhetoric. Once more, in this book, Naipaul makes individual people bring the dilemmas of Pakistan to life. A shrewd businessman pours out the history of the pre-Aryan race of Sind (creators of the Indus valley civilisation) 'in one gulp'. He was agonised by dreams of fortune; haunted by general dishonesty. The beauty of Islam, he says, lay in its mixture of law and compassion and in its charity. He recommended the author to the shrines of Sind.

At the end, with a tenderness for which I wasn't prepared, he pressed his forefinger to the middle of my forehead. He said, 'That is where it gets you. If you were a businessman you would get blood pressure. You're an intellectual. You are concerned with the truth. So it gets you there, in the eyes. You must rest your eyes. You must look at green things.'

Several of Naipaul's acquaintances remarked on the tired look of his harassed eyes. There was relief for him when he went up to the Kaghan valley in sight of the Himalayas with a science student called Masood. They saw the migrating Afghan shepherds – one of the spectacles of this part of the world – where 'the busy little trotters of the sheep ground the fine dust of the road finer'. This long chapter is indeed the most refreshing in the book, largely of course because we are out of the conflicts of the cities far below where the mixture of old and new is grotesque to the point of vulgarity. Here the effect was of tribal gorgeousness and the certainty of usage and tradition in everyday things:

> One woman walked with one shoe on, the other off, and on her head. It was a style – the shoe on the head: later we saw women with both shoes on their heads, the heels fitted one into another to form a little arch. Shoes were worn when the ground was pebbly; when the ground was smooth or soft with dust it was better to walk barefooted.

To Malaysia, Islam had spread from India and Pakistan as an idea. There had been no planting of Arab colonies, no sending back of treasure and slaves and, up to now, religion was simply the old village tradition. Now that has changed: Islamic missionaries from Pakistan bring in the sense of a world movement: the village Muslims now feel the awakened rage of passive pastoral people against the rich in the towns, above all the incessantly active Chinese. There were leaders of the younger generation who had been to England for education, one to Bradford. He disapproved of Bradford. The people there 'are too individualistic . . . They're trying to say be together with others, but not with your family. They are created by their own technology.' Modern Malaysia must not copy that. Free-mixing of the sexes, the use of alcohol are the great

Western evils. There were 'brave' independent girls here, but they had covered hair. The face may be seen, but the hands only from the wrist. What did the girls read in their English classes? Thomas Hardy! But, more avidly, Barbara Cartland, Perry Mason, James Hadley Chase. This is pretty comedy. More serious is Shafi, the guide and mentor who – like Behzad – loved a long quiet soul-searching. He had first lost his village, travelled to America and then had lost the last of his traditions. 'I could see how, without Islam,' Naipaul says, 'he would be lost.' Shafi was trying to run a Muslim commune. Was it possible to be close to Nature without exploiting it? he anxiously enquired. An ecologist might sympathise.

When Naipaul gets to Indonesia he finds a people stunned by foreign occupations, by memories of the massacres of 1965 and now, clamped under Army rule – like people 'looking, from a distance, at a mysterious part of themselves'. Islam was the formal faith, but below that were relics of the Hindu-Buddhist animist past, 'no longer part of a system'. The reader himself cannot hold in his mind the world Mr Naipaul asks us to see in a new light, but his strength lies in the tense pitch of his enquiry and in his narrative that brings people and landscape to life in flashes of telling detail, and gives them meaning as, also self-portrayed, he passes through.

George Orwell

THE CRYSTAL SPIRIT

The eccentric, the crank, and the thorn in the flesh turn up regularly in British life and in war many of them come into their own. This was certainly true of George Orwell, who, in addition, was two persons: the suppressed figure of Eric Blair, once a police officer in Burma, old Etonian, and poor Scot, briefly soldier of misfortune in the Spanish Civil War; and George Orwell, amateur outcast, Bohemian, and journalist who, as Herbert Read said, raised journalism to the dignity of literature. He was a familiar London figure in BBC circles during World War II – he was in charge of broadcasts to India – in the Soho pubs, the offices of *Horizon*, and in many districts where poor writers settled in those hungry and seedy times. There is considerable Orwell anecdotage. It was impossible to know such a complex, straying, and contradictory man well, but George Woodcock, who became a friend after the usual quarrel which established one with Orwell, gives a good account of his personal spell, and has written a very penetrating personal study.

Orwell looked, as Mr Woodcock says, like Don Quixote and he was haunted by his Sancho Panza; better still, like a 'frayed sahib' in shabby jacket and corduroy and betraying his class by his insouciance. Tall and bony, the face lined with pain, eyes that stared out of their caves, he looked far away over one's head as if seeking more comfort and new indignations. He had a thin-lipped, hard mouth; his general bleakness was relieved by sudden smiles and by a vigorous shock of wiry hair *en brosse*. The voice had the lazy, almost spiritless, Cockney drawl, but had something like a rusty edge to it that suggested trouble and had been used to authority. He seemed more at home than we were in the bleak no-man's-land that war creates in the mind and in life in general.

[96]

Among my encounters with him three stand out. I once went back to a half-empty flat he had taken on the top floor of a high and once expensive block of flats in St John's Wood. He pointed out that the building was half empty because of the Blitz, the rents had dropped low, and that it was lucky to be able to live close to the roof because you could get out quickly to deal with the fire-bombs. He seemed to want to live as near to a bomb as possible. Another time we stood for a long time in a doorway off Piccadilly while he told me about the advantage of keeping goats in the country with full details of cost and yield – for he was a born small-holder and liked manual work. While at the BBC he spent his evenings in a part-time job making small parts for aircraft. He tried to get me to bring my family and join him in the disastrous migration to the island of Jura. The attraction of the island seemed to be that it was out of touch with the mainland for long periods because of storms, that one would be scrabbling along the rocks and shores for food and fuel, and would be free of the competition of modern totalitarianism. We were eating and drinking expensively and well in Percy Street at the time, for a genial Sancho Panza would unexpectedly take over from the gaunt Quixote. One of the things that made him hate industrial capitalism was that it fed its people so badly on the ersatz and had so demoralised them that they could not cook. But, at the same time, he would stuff his pipe with cheap shag bought at miserable little shops and drink strong tea out of its saucer – in the romantic belief that this was what the decent British workman did, and point out the moral advantages of dossing down in 'working-class discomfort'.

These habits led to charges of affectation. Certainly there was a streak of moral vanity in Orwell; but, as Mr Woodcock says, the charge of affectation is superficial. There was an element of inverted dandyism in Orwell and it is indicated by his surprising admiration for Oscar Wilde and especially for Dorian Gray. Orwell was not at all interested in homosexuality but he was fascinated by Dorian's double personality and his impulse to go native in his own country. The other statement, made at the time of his death, was that his opting out of our kind of society, and his eagerness to suffer – as in the harsh experience in Jura – were suicidal. He was already tubercular. It is true that there seemed to be a core of exhausted indifference or something like a gambler's neutrality of spirit in him; but the belief that one could find the comely, natural life in primitive surroundings among simple people was central to him. 'Comeliness' was one of his favourite words. He certainly would not have taken the adopted son, whom he adored, on an expedition directed to a suicide. We cannot know much about this because Orwell insisted that no biography should be written about him. He was secretive and liked to keep his friends and his life in different compartments.

It is well known that Orwell's political conscience and interests were precocious and that his ideas grew out of action. He was closer to Camus, Silone, and Koestler than he was to any English contemporaries who were not blind to Continental politics but hated to believe they were real. He had resigned from the Burmese police on principle, but unlike many romantic rebels, he respected the need for authority, as one can see in the passages where he defended Kipling. In many ways, the Radical was conservative – as English radicals have often been. For him, Victorian colonialism and Victorian England were bad, but, at any rate, concealed a core of personal decency. This, he believed, would have little chance of surviving in our period of disintegration in which we were bent on saving ourselves through an authority that was impersonal, totalitarian, non-human, and dishonest. We were condemned to Newspeak.

Orwell's pictures of England are a mixture of sarcasm, pragmatism, and sentiment. One must treat his writings as one treats Shaw's: collect the fragments of good sense. The Burmese experience led him to suppose, as Mr Woodcock says, that the attitude of the colonial rulers to ruled was identical with the attitude of the English and European ruling class to its workers. They were outcasts too and he sought to join them. This diagnosis was extravagant and his personal renunciation led him to meet outcasts only, the down-and-outs. In this he was as romantic as Dorian Gray. For the main body of the British working class have been respectable and self-respecting since the industrial revolution. They were educated by their unions. The class barrier was absolute on their side. Their obsession with sport, beer, gambling, and bad newspapers did not affect their tenacious political puritanism. They too, like Orwell – this is their one link with him – had a double mind; but they were not *déclassés*. In his

[98]

slapdash book about English life, *The Lion and the Unicorn*, he made a tolerably good picture of the truculent and lazy-minded English muddle.

The value of Mr Woodcock's study lies in the care with which he picks his way among Orwell's self-contradictions and follows his progress from work to work. This is a difficult task, for Orwell was not one for organised abstract thought. He is as drastic but as variable as a Cobbett or a Dickens – even, it has lately struck me – as Carlyle. His essay on Dickens is about the best thing done by an English writer since Gissing. It is important to understand how seriously Orwell worked at finding a style that would reflect his attempt at a *natural* attitude to his subjects, his curious humour, and his realism. From the coloured uncertainties and guesses of journalism, he advanced to a prose as clear as rain, Swift-like in passages of *Homage to Catalonia* and *Animal Farm*. Mr Woodcock is very interesting on the links between the early *Burmese Days* (the work of liberation), the childhood passages in *Coming Up for Air*, and the fantasies in *1984*; and in the sadistic images which crop up mysteriously. It is also instructive to see how his interest in the abuse of language grew from his work in the BBC. He was not a good novelist, but he was 'in life' and an intrepid pamphleteer.

John Osborne

A BETTER CLASS OF PERSON

━━━━━━━

John Osborne has always been a master of spoken diatribe, whether it is of the 'bloody but unbowed' kind or the picturesque confessional of wounds given and received. In his vigorous autobiography *A Better Class of Person* he has the wound-licking grin of the only child who has been through the class mill and is getting his own back – very much a comic Mr Polly or a Kipps reborn in 1929, if less sunny and innocent than Wells was. Osborne adds to the rich tradition of English low comedy, which draws on the snobberies and vulgarities of lower-middle-class life, with its guts, its profligate will to survive despite its maudlin or self-pitying streak. He calls his people Edwardian, for manners drag on long after their presumed historical death; really his family were on the bohemian verges. Both the Welsh and the Cockney sides – the latter known in the family folklore as 'the Tottenham Crowd', with some sniffing of the nose – had a racy leaning towards pubs, music halls, and theatre. (All, except his sad father, lived to a tremendous age.) His two grandfathers were well-established if secretive rakes; one was the manager of a once famous London pub in the theatre district and had an early-morning spat with the lavishly seductive Marie Lloyd. Osborne's Welsh father was a self-taught pianist who could sing a song. He earned his living as an advertising copywriter of sorts until his health collapsed. He first met Nellie Beatrice Grove, who was to be the playwright's mother, when she was a barmaid in the Strand. She had left school at twelve to scrub floors in an orphanage, had quickly bettered herself as a cashier in a Lyons Corner House, and eventually went on to the bar of a suburban hotel. She resented her sister Queenie putting on airs because she had, by some family accident, been 'educated' and worked in a milliner's. (The class struggle has its nuances.)

If one uncle was a stoker in the Navy, another had an admired connection with Abdulla cigarettes. Was he a director? Goodness knows, but he smoked the expensive things all day. Bids for gentility were natural in a family that, on both sides, took some pride in having 'come down in the world'. Osborne writes:

> ... the Groves seemed to feel less sense of grievance, looking on it as the justified price of profligate living or getting above yourself, rather than as a cruel trick of destiny ... They had a litany of elliptical sayings, almost biblical in their complexity, which, to the meanest mind or intelligence, combined accessibility and authority. Revealed family wisdom was expressed in sayings like, 'One door opens and another one always shuts' (the optimistic version – rare – was the same in reverse). 'I think I can say I've had my share of sorrows.' Like Jesus they were all acquainted with grief. 'I can always read him like a book'; 'I've never owed anyone anything' (almost the Family Motto this), 'You can't get round him, he's like a Jew and his cash box'; 'Look at him, like Lockhart's elephant.'

The last was a characteristic piece of poetic fancy by which the Londoner draws on local history. The words meant that someone was relating the young Osborne to times before his own; he was 'clumsy'. The elephant evoked a popular large bun sold at a cheap and now extinct eating-house in the Strand. I believe the American equivalent would be Child's.

Osborne was an only child, and for long years he was too sickly to be sent to school. No adult spoke to him much, so he listened, puzzling his way through the family babble. Religion was remote. Comfort in the discomfort of others, he remarks, was the abiding family recreation. 'Disappointment,' Osborne adds, 'was oxygen to them.' The Family Row at Christmas was an institution, the Groves shouting, the Osbornes calmer and more bitter in their sense of having been cheated at birth. Nellie Beatrice, the barmaid mother, mangled the language with her Tottenham mispronunciations – very upsetting to the precise and eloquent Welsh. As she complained, they 'passed looks' when she spoke. Her genius shone at the bar:

Quick, anticipative with a lightning head for mental arithmetic, she was, as she put it, a very smart 'licensed victualler's assistant' indeed. '*I'm* not a barmaid I'm a victualler's assistant – *if* you please.' I have seen none better. No one could draw a pint with a more perfect head on it or pour out four glasses of beer at the same time, throwing bottles up in the air and catching them as she did so.

She was known as Bobby, and was noted for shouting out her wartime catch phrases: 'Get up them stairs'; 'The second thing he did when he come home was to take his pack off'; or 'I couldn't laugh if I was crafty.' At home, her energies were restless. She was a relentless cleaner, whether she lived in digs in dreary Fulham or in a snobby suburb, and never stopped stripping and cleaning the few rooms they lived in, taking up all the carpets and taking down all curtains once a week. She loved moving house. Meals, such as they were, were made to be washed up rather than to be eaten. She was a mistress of the black look. She was hungry for glamour, not for bringing up children, and certainly not a sickly boy who caught every illness going. Her ideal – after the father died and the war filled her purse with wartime tips – was to 'go Up West', walk round the big London stores without buying anything, complaining of her feet, and have a lunch at the gaudy Trocadero, where she could look suitably stand-offish. She was deeply respectable. This is the half-cruel portrait by her son, who was to become a 'better class of person'. He confesses to a struggle against a shame of her:

> My mother's hair was very dark, occasionally hennaed. Her face was a floury dark mask, her eyes were an irritable brown, her ears small, so unlike her father's ('He's got Satan's ears, he has'), her nose surprisingly fine. Her remaining front teeth were large, yellow, and strong. Her lips were a scarlet-black sliver covered in some sticky slime named Tahiti or Tattoo, which she bought with all her other make-up from Woolworth's. She wore it, or something like it, from the beginning of the First World War onwards. She had a cream base called Crème Simone, always covered up with a face powder called Tokalon, which she dabbed all over so that it almost showered off in little avalanches when she leant forward over her food. This was all topped off by a

kind of knicker-bocker glory of rouge, which came in rather pretty little blue and white boxes – again from Woolworth's – and looked like a mixture of blackcurrant juice and brick dust. The final coup was an overgenerous dab of California Poppy, known to schoolboys as 'fleur de dustbins'.

What froze him was that she was incurious about him.
The frail short-lived father had been white-haired since his twenties.

His skin was extremely pale, almost transparent. He had the whitest hands I think I have ever seen; Shalimar hands he called them. ('Pale hands I love beside the Lethe waters', of Shalimar. It was one of his favourite Sunday ballads.)

But his long fingers were stained by nicotine. His clothes were unpressed and his bowler hat and mac were greasy, but he was particular about his cuffs and collars and his highly polished, papery shoes. A gentle, sad creature, he is oddly described as being like a 'Welsh-sounding prurient, reticent investigator of sorts from a small provincial town'. For some reason unknown – not only because of his long spells in hospital – the couple were mostly apart.

For the only child, schools were places of pain and humiliation. Certainly they were often rough. He had to discover cunning. At one mixed school, the adolescent girls turned out to be the thumping bullies of the smaller boys, preparing them for the sex war. Still, in the suburbs, there were sympathetic, literate families who helped the backward autodidact. He was nothing more than a nuisance to his energetic mother, and by now they almost hated one another. He was luckier than he thinks to be sent to a third-rate boarding school, for he did at least read a lot and did pretty well with his belated education. But he was laughed at for saying he wanted to be a historian and go to a university. All he was fit for, he was told, was journalism. He was sacked for hitting a master who had slapped him and for writing love-letters to a girl there. Schools took a stern line on that. The sexual revolution, though rife elsewhere, did not easily penetrate the semi-genteel regions of provincial life. So journalism it was. The Benevolent Society to which his father had subscribed and which had paid for his schooling completed its obligations by getting him introduced to a publisher who produced trade journals like the *Gas World*. He had to prepare himself for this by going to typing and shorthand classes.

Folly is often a salvation in such dreary circumstances. Osborne was eighteen, spotty, shy, and longing for friends, especially girls. It occurred to him that a course of dancing lessons at a school that put on amateur theatricals was a likely chance. He became a dim star and sent his photograph to a theatrical agent; the bohemian traits of his upbringing sprang up in his sullen, slightly flashy being. He had first to disentangle himself from the usual sentimental suburban engagement to a nice enough girl who took her reluctant boyfriend (earning two pounds a week) to the windows of furniture shops. The warning was clear. He jilted her, wrote her remorseful, high-minded letters, was tormented by guilt and by threats and denunciations from the parents. But he was soon out on tour with a third-rate company and learned about theatre without training from the bottom, starting with the job of assistant stage-manager and understudying the five actors, aged between twenty-five and seventy. What is clear from the long picaresque experiences with this down-at-heel and hungry company is that he was really a writer and, despite poetising ambitions, had a marvellous ear for real speech. The book is punctuated by passages from his plays that hark back to what he heard 'on the road'. The 'real' life is in fact the overflow of theatrical life evoking people outside. On that first long tour, sexually starved, he simpered after a fluttering actress called Sheila but soon had the simper knocked out of him by a formidable actress called Stella, an aggressive thirty-year-old, with 'the shoulders of a Channel swimmer' and a body that 'looked capable of snapping up an intruder in a jawbone of flesh'. She was 'arrogantly lubricious' and had 'an almost masculine, stalking power'. She was not put off by by his sickly appearance and his acne; she expertly detected the writer in him, and was after him to revise his first attempt as a collaborator, on a play that she and her husband wanted to put on. When she and Osborne became lovers, they quarrelled incessantly about dramatic construction; she was out for the commercial success of another *Autumn Crocus* or *Dinner at Eight* – what he calls 'a Nice Play' about middle-class gatherings. She in fact woke up his independent intelligence. He discovered he had his own ideas about the theatre. She said he was a lazy, arrogant, dishonest amateur – not only that but ungrateful to her complaisant husband, who tolerantly rescued them when the company's run stopped and the money ran out. She had to take a job as a waitress and Osborne became a dishwasher. She eventually left him for a job in the North, and he admits that he spitefully left her door unlocked and her electricity turned on when he left the flat she had lent him. Rightly, she never forgave him. Years later, the play did run for a week, with Osborne trying to recognise some lines of his own in it.

The knockabout theatrical chapters tend to be repetitive, but they are rich in sharp, short portraits, especially of the theatrical landladies. They end with his runaway marriage with one Pamela, a capable young actress. He was tactless enough to carry on this passion when the company got to her own home town, in the face of her hostile family. They were well-established drapers. The correlative scripture of what went on in real life will be seen in the quotations from *Look Back in Anger*, notably Jimmy Porter's speech about the wedding:

Mummy was slumped over her pew in a heap – the noble, female rhino, pole-axed at last! And Daddy sat beside her, upright and unafraid, dreaming of his days among the Indian Princes, and unable to believe he'd left his horsewhip at home.

Osborne says that this is a fairly accurate account of the wedding, except for the references to the Indian Princes. They seem unlikely in the life of a local draper. Daddy has in fact been elevated socially by the 'angry' exposer of class consciousness. Osborne is safer as a guide to congealed suburban or theatrical snobberies. He now writes about the episode:

I was aware that I had left behind the sophistication and tolerance of the true provinces. Sprung from Fulham and Stoneleigh, where feelings rarely rose higher than a black look, the power of place, family, and generation in small towns was new to me. In the suburbs, allegiances are lost or discarded on dutifully paid visits. The present kept itself to

[105]

itself. In such a life there was no common graveyard for memory or future. The suburb has no graveyard.

Just before the end of the book there is a collection of extracts from Nellie Beatrice's letters. Years have passed, but she's still on the move, saving up gift stamps for a new carpet-shampoo cleaner, washing down the ceiling, though 'I never did like Housework'. She just wanted things clean. And then comes her crushing phrase:

> I'll say that for him – he's never been *ashamed* of me. He's always let me meet his friends – and they're all theatrical people, a good class all of them, they speak nicely.

And to his notebook Osborne groans:

> I am ashamed of her as part of myself that can't be cast out, my own conflict, the disease which I suffer and have inherited, what I *am* and never could be whole.

About that time, 1955, George Devine rowed out to Osborne, who was living on a barge on the Thames, and offered him a twenty-pound option on *Look Back in Anger*. English theatre changed in a night. I look forward to Volume Two.

Walker Percy

CLOWNS

The hero as the clown. It is not a new idea, but it can be given a new twist if he is sick and if the 'normal' world is more absurd, more dangerous, and sicker than he is. *That* sickness comes from the normal man's refusal to face the facts; the clown's sickness comes from a morbid awareness of them. Having gone through so much, he is clever and stoical. He pesters himself to the point of laughter. After all, he is the comedian of the clinic; and, in Walker Percy's novels, the clinic is sex-mad, science-mad, pleasure-mad contemporary life.

Why is the clown sick? After reading *Love in the Ruins*, which is a satirical fantasy set in the United States twenty or thirty years ahead, one sees that the basic reasons have been developed since that very seductive first novel, *The Movie-goer*. In this work the clown is a prosperous young broker and lapsed Catholic in New Orleans, pursuing happiness in the civilisation which has stretched that piece of elastic until it snaps back on him. Caught by the itch for instant sex, new things, and the general go-go, he is unaccountably trapped by malaise. Buy a new car, try a new girl, and there is the instant 'pain of loss'. He is no longer 'more able to be in the world than Banquo's ghost'. He becomes 'abstracted from reality' and can be said to be 'orbiting in limbo' between 'angelism and bestiality'. In *The Movie-goer*, he is a nice, clever, unreliable young man. The movie ideal of the car and the girl never quite works:

> . . . I discovered to my dismay that my fine new Dodge was a regular incubator of malaise. Though it was comfortable enough, though it ran like a clock, though we went spinning along in perfect comfort and with a perfect view of the scenery like the American couple in the

Dodge ad, the malaise quickly became suffocating. We sat frozen in a gelid amiability. Our cheeks ached from smiling. Either would have died for the other. In despair I put my hand under her dress, but even such a homely little gesture as that was received with the same fearful politeness. I longed to stop the car and bang my head against the curb. We were free, moreover, to do that or anything else, but instead on we rushed, a little vortex of despair moving through the world like the still eye of a hurricane.

In *The Last Gentleman*, the sense of loss becomes literal amnesia. He has lost identity, but that is rooted of course in the past and there, somewhere lying about, was the religion he no longer believes in; also the security of a shady but settled way of life in the South. To devote oneself blindly to another's pain is worth a try; but shy of a moral so schematic, he turns this into a wandering adventure all the way from New York to Louisiana with the bizarre family of a dying youth. The sick make good picaresque figures, for sickness gives one the sharp eyes and freedom of fever.

Walker Percy's gift is for moving about, catching the smell of locality, and for a laughing enjoyment between his bouts with desperation and loss. As in pretty well all intelligent American novels, the sense of America as an effluence of bizarre locality is strong. The hero is liable to sexual hay fever. This book ends with him racing after his sinful psychiatrist, in desperation. Case unsolved, but he has travelled like mad, his eyes starting out of his head: a comedian.

In *Love in the Ruins*, the sick hero is older. He is in his disgraceful forties, a brilliant alcoholic and girl-chasing doctor, liable to depression and bowel trouble most of the week. But war and general disaster have an appeasing or stimulating effect upon neurotics. The sense of a loss beyond his own wakes up his eccentric faculties; now he sees that the world is more farcical than he is. For the America of (I suppose) the 1990s is breaking up. There have been outbreaks of civil war for years, brought on by Negro risings and the fifteen-year war in Ecuador:

For our beloved old U.S.A. is in a bad way. Americans have turned against each other; race against race, right against left, believer against heathen, San Francisco against Los Angeles, Chicago against Cicero. Vines sprout in sections of New York where not even Negroes will live. Wolves have been seen in downtown Cleveland . . .

Poison ivy grows up the speaker-posts in drive-in movies, vegetation grows through the cracks in the highways, and – greatest of all symbols of disaster – many a Howard Johnson motel has gone up in flames. Of course there has been nuclear fallout here and there. The hero has hives.

A disastrous story, but not very tragic for the doctor, although his wife has run off with an English Buddhist and his daughter has died. A shrewd irony, helped by a mixture of bourbon and self-interest, pulls him together. Not only that: he is lucky to live in a suburban town which survives in a state of respectable paranoia on the edge of a swamp inhabited by murderers and other disaffected people. Occasionally the murderers come out for the kill, but golf staggers along. In the Fedvil complex, the hospital still stands, the Masters-and-Johnson-style Love Clinic – now run by a lapsed Irish priest – is packed every day with experimental copulators who earn fifty dollars a go; the Geriatric Rehab buildings keep people alive until they are a hundred, and euthanasia does well at Happy Isles. You press the Euphoria button.

The American way carries on, but the evasions, the unaccountable rages, and the tendency to be abstracted from reality and orbit in limbo and to alternate between bits of meaningless idealism and bestiality have increased. Cunningly the doctor has patched up a corner of a wrecked Howard Johnson where he plans to store three girls he will save in the next wave of destruction. Sniping has begun again, there are rumours of a new rising of blacks, and there is a sodium cloud in the distance.

The doctor, known to be a crackpot genius and no more than a nuisance when in drink, has a consolation. The study of sodium and encephalology has led him in the course of years to create an instrument called the lapsometer. It measures the electrical activity of the separate centres of the brain. Can the readings be correlated with the causes of the woes of the Western World, its terrors, rages, and impulses, even the perturbations of the soul? Up to a point they can be. There are comic successes with the impotent, the frigid, the angry, the passive: the medical comedy is very good. The hospital suspects the metaphysical turn of its drunk genius, but the Director sees what a political weapon the lapsometer can be. What a gift for Washington, this machine that can, at any rate, manipulate people if it can do no more.

This theme of science fiction is crossed with the drama of the community's situation. The riots are beginning, murders increase, the sodium cloud comes nearer, the sand in the golf bunkers is on fire. Saved by his lapsed Presbyterian secretary, the lapsed Catholic stays on in the wrecked community, now largely taken over by the blacks who copy English accents from their English golf pros on the course. The intellectual blacks have fled to Berkeley, Harvard, and the University of Michigan, to scowl at the mixed-up population who, as well as they can, get on with ordinary life. The doctor is nearly off the bottle and nearly off chasing girls.

To satirise the present one pretends it is the future. Mr Walker Percy's present is limbo; a scene of wicked comedy, sharp portraits of types, and awful habits of mind. The religious and political mix-up is very funny. He is a spirited and inventive writer and there is a charred hell-fire edge to his observation. Exactly what, as a moralist, he wants us to do, I'm not sure. Join the remains of the church, get back to the doctor's ancestor Sir Thomas More? Or simply rejoin ordinary life? Or is middle age the ideal to be aimed at? He is more interested in the state of sex than in the state of the Union: but isn't sex just the latest item of conspicuous waste in Western society? I am afraid that in the eye of this hurricane of laughing anger, there is a sentimentalist. Still, a very clever one, full of ideas. As always in American novels, the impedimenta are good. Sears Roebuck has made its contribution to literature.

Forrest Reid

ESCAPING FROM BELFAST

Early in 1923, when I was a very naïve and untrained newspaper correspondent in Dublin, it was my duty to take a regular trip to Belfast and to find out what was going on politically in that depressing and bigoted city of linen mills and shipyards. The Orangemen were contemptuous of the Southern Irish and had a blustering condescension to Englishmen like myself, and one of the few people whose talk was a relief from this was Forrest Reid, a novelist and critic in his late forties, admired by Yeats, Forster and Walter de la Mare, but almost ignored in his own city at that time.

His family had belonged to the merchant class, who were relatively free of the political stubbornness which was extreme among the industrialists and their workers. He himself was totally indifferent to Irish or to any other brand of politics. He had broken with the Christian faith and was a professed pagan of the Classical Greek persuasion – certainly without the Gaelic nostalgia of the South, despite his friendship with Yeats. I found him living alone on the top floor of a shabby house in a noisy and dirty factory district. His room was bare and poor, and only packed shelves of books, carefully bound in white paper covers to protect them from smoke and smuts, suggested the bibliophile and the scholar. A pile of novels for review stood on his table, alongside his papers and pencils, and the remains of a cold leg of mutton which, I imagined, had to last the week, and during our talks he would sit near to a miserable little fire, shyly drawing intricate patterns with a poker in the soot on the back of the fireplace. I had never met a book-reviewer before, had not read any of his novels, and though by this time I had heard talk of mysticism, the supernatural, visions, and of reality dissolving into dreams, these subjects were above my head and beyond my inclination.

[111]

But his talk was quiet and enlightening. He did once or twice mention that E. M. Forster was a friend of his and that he knew Cambridge, and this explained why his speech was free of the mournful glottal-bottle blurting of Ulster address; as I had not heard of Forster at the time, this made Reid even stranger to me. The certainty was that he was one more example of the 'quare fellow' or of the large population of Ireland's eternal bachelors. He was forty-eight. I left Ireland, and not until years later, when I read *Apostate*, the account of his upbringing in Belfast, did I understand that he was more than a shabby and kindly eccentric schoolmasterish man. He was ugly in a fascinating way because of his high block-like forehead and his broad nose that turned up at the tip as if in ironic inquiry, but there was a kind of genius in his truthful portraits of boys as the wary or daring young animal grows up.

His present biographer mentions that Reid's small feet had high insteps, which – to me, at any rate – suggests someone capable of springing into some other air. I had not noticed his feet, nor did I know that this lonely and engaging man was a pederast – one who found the homosexual and heterosexual acts 'disgusting' and who had sublimated his desires in tutorial friendships that, perforce, would die as those he loved grew up, got tired of him or married – the last hard for him to bear.

An earlier biographer of Forrest Reid – Russell Burlingham – found this subject difficult to discuss in 1953. So, even now, does Brian Taylor, but he has treated it with delicacy and understanding. If Forrest Reid was 'a case', Taylor shows that 'a case' is in itself a crude simplification of life. All 'cases' are different: Reid was an instance of the man whose desires are overruled by his affections and his principles. He spoke frankly of his 'arrested development', and, as Taylor shows, it led to a lifelong preoccupation with the intervention of dream-like moments in reality. As a youth – in Belfast of all places – he had been under the influence of Henry James to the point of writing to the Master boldly and getting flattering replies. As for the 'pagan supernatural', that had been stimulated by Forster's *The Celestial Omnibus* and the stories and poems of Walter de la Mare. The latter pair had become his literary counsellors and friends. He rather daringly sent his first novel to Henry James, who responded seriously: but when the Master read Reid's second novel, *The Garden God*,

based on an incident noted by Reid in which the portrait of a beautiful
boy by G. A. Storey in the Royal Academy dissolves, and the boy turns
into a phantom dressed in a silver suit riding in a forest, so that 'something
told me that I was looking on either the boy's innermost life, or on some
former life of his', James was embarrassed and angered by the platonic
eroticism of the book and broke off the relationship in a panic. Edmund
Gosse was not disturbed. He detected the pain in Reid's isolation and
added that 'for people too obstinately *themselves*, there is always dream-
land'. A rather Barrie-like observation: but if Reid was timid and not
without self-pity, he was not a sentimentalist. He found a complex
resource in a Proustian obsession with memory, and a curiosity about
Time. In one of his much-praised later novels, *Uncle Stephen*, there is a
passage:

> *Could* you be in two times at once? Certainly your mind could be in
> one time and your body in another . . . Somebody might come to you
> of *his* time into yours. You might, for instance, come face to face with
> your own father as he was when he was a boy. Of course you wouldn't
> *know* each other: still you might meet and become friends, the way you
> do with people in dreams.

Reid seems to be stating, as Brian Taylor suggests, 'his perennial concern
with a boy's search for a father, a childless man's search for a son, and
the reaching out of both for companionship and understanding'.

Forrest Reid was the youngest and not much wanted son of a Belfast
merchant whose business was failing and of a mother of an old aristocratic
English family who could not conceal that she had married beneath her.
This story is told in *Apostate*. Reid's passionate love was given totally to
his nurse, Emma, who after a few years left home: he could love no
woman after that. After his father's early death, the family went further
down hill, the neglected boy played with 'rough' boys in the streets and
was a pain to his older sisters. He was ugly, but his boyish animal spirits
were high and he was clever. He left a good school early and was put to
work in a tea merchant's office, an easy trade, for he found it simple to
hide in a storeroom and read Greek and was determined to write. In
loneliness, his search for friendships was fierce and possessive. He was

already a Platonist. His mother's death freed him from the tea trade, for he was left a small legacy, and, at last, got what he wanted – a place at Cambridge – but far too late. (He was nearly thirty and said he got little out of his time there.) He can be said to have been penned in by autobiography all his life, writing version after version of his boyhood experience, in nearly all his novels, and becoming obsessed about 'getting it right' while evading – as was inevitable in his time – the sexual dilemma. Perhaps the pagan did not quite suppress the Presbyterian, and he was left, as he said, 'intractable' in his companionship with the one or two men with whom he lived in a tutor–pupil relationship.

The striking things in Reid's writing are the clarity of his descriptive style, his fervid response to landscape and his totally unsentimental, almost minute-to-minute evocations of the changes in a boy's real and imaginative experience as he passes from childhood to youth and the loss of wild innocence. He recalls what the day brought and felt like without affectation and what most of us have inevitably generalised or forgotten in growing up. We have forgotten, also, the passing dreams that suddenly came and abruptly vanished. His obsession, or perhaps a half-humorous pedantry, obliged him to try and try again exactly to recover those moments – which of course narrowed his scope – and the many quotations here from scenes in his novels and from his letters make this point. One is especially struck by the curious fact that Aksakoff's memories of *his* childhood under the rule of a dominant mother was one of Reid's favourite books – one more example of a natural sympathy between some Irish writing and the Russian feeling for the vivid and troubled hour of the day. The pagan Greek ideal has something precious and Ninetyish in it, and this Russian naturalness seems to me a more valuable influence on his talent, although Reid's Irishness was almost non-existent, except in that pure, direct response to the natural scene, whereas Aksakoff's Russianness was historically Slavophil and innate.

Reid has been thought of as a provincial and escapist: he accepted that. He wrote in a letter that he 'preferred the literature of escape and what *I* should call the literature of imagination for the escape is only from the impermanent into the permanent'. Brian Taylor refers to Russell Burlingham's *Forrest Reid: A Portrait and a Study* for purely literary criticism.

Taylor's is a sensitive and intelligent study of Reid's dilemma without the dramatising aid of Freudian or sociological fictions. As a person, Reid becomes very clear, sad and droll. He was soon to leave that bare room where I first listened to his talk and his friendly silences. He moved to a council house outside Belfast with his adored dogs and his current friend, perpetuating a kind of boyhood, smoking his pipe as though he were a Belfast chimney. He could be testy at the card-table. He was barricaded by an ever-growing pile of first editions, he pondered his stamp collection, and was loftily resigned to being more avidly read for his excellent book reviews than – as far as the large public was concerned – for his admired and not very saleable novels. He did attain a local fame. One claim he could make: the scrupulous artist had reserves of sudden extrovert fierceness and triumphant skill and cunning – he could win Challenge Cups at croquet all over England and Ireland. No sublimation there: he was certain to get through those hoops.

Salman Rushdie

MIDNIGHT'S CHILDREN

In Salman Rushdie, the author of *Midnight's Children* (Jonathan Cape, 1981), India has produced a great novelist – one with startling imaginative and intellectual resources, a master of perpetual storytelling. Like Marquez in *One Hundred Years of Solitude*, he weaves a whole people's capacity for carrying its inherited myths – and new ones that it goes on generating – into a kind of magic carpet. The human swarm swarms in every man and woman as they make their bid for life and vanish into the passion or hallucination that hangs about them like the smell of India itself. Yet at the same time there are Western echoes, particularly of the irony of Sterne in *Tristram Shandy* – that early non-linear writer – in Rushdie's readiness to tease by breaking off or digressing in the gravest moments. This is very odd in an Indian novel! The book is really about the mystery of being born. Rushdie's realism is that of the conjuror who, in a flash, draws an incident out of the air and then makes it vanish and laughs at his cleverness. A pregnant woman, the narrator's mother, goes to a fortune-teller in the Delhi slum:

> And my mother's face, rabbit-startled, watching the prophet in the check shirt as he began to circle, his eyes still egglike in the softness of his face; and suddenly a shudder passing through him and again that strange high voice as the words issued through his lips (I must describe those lips, too – but later, because now . . .) 'A son.'
>
> Silent cousins – monkeys on leashes, ceasing their chatter – cobras coiled in baskets – and the circling fortune-teller, finding history speaking through his lips.

And the fortune-teller goes on, sing-songing:

> 'Washing will hide him – voices will guide him! Friends mutilate him
> – blood will betray him . . . jungle will claim him . . . tyrants will fry
> him . . . He will have sons without having sons! He will be old before
> he is old! *And he will die . . . before he is dead.*'

Outside the room, monkeys are throwing down stones on the street from
a ruined building.

This is pure *Arabian Nights* intrigue – for that son, Saleem Sinai, now
thirty-one, is writing about what he is making up about his birth; he is
dramatising his past life as a prophecy, even universalising his history as
a mingling of farce and horror and matching it with thirty years of the
Indian crowd's collective political history. The strength of a book that
might otherwise be a string of picaresque tales lies in its strong sense of
design. Saleem claims that it is he who has created modern India in the
years that followed Indian independence – has dreamed into being the
civil strife and the wars – as a teller of stories, true or untrue, conniving
at events and united with them. Central to this is the fantasy that the
children born at midnight on the day of liberation, as he was, have a
destiny. The Prime Minister himself pronounces this: 'They are the seed
of a future that would genuinely differ from anything that the world had
seen at that time.' Children born a few seconds before the hour of what
Saleem calls Mountbatten's 'tick-tock' are likely to join the revelling band
of conjurors and circus freaks and street singers; those born a few seconds
after midnight, like Parvati, the witch, whom Saleem eventually marries,
will be genuine sorcerers. Saleem himself, born on the stroke of the hour,
will be amazingly gifted but will also embody the disasters of the country.
The novel is an autobiography, dictated by a ruined man to a simple but
shrewd working girl in a pickle factory – to this Saleem's fortunes have
fallen. (She is addressed from time to time as if she were Sterne's 'dear
Eliza'.) The fortune-teller's words 'washing will hide him' point to Fate.
The prophecy was not a joke.

The rich Delhi Muslims who raise him are not his parents: he is a
changeling, and not their son. The wrong ticket has been tied to his toe
by a poor Goanese nurse, who, demented by the infidelity of her husband,

a common street singer, had allowed herself to be seduced by a departing English sahib. Saleem is ugly, dwarfish, with a huge snotty nose, and is brought up rich; the real son is Shiva, brought up poor. Years will pass before the nurse confesses. The point of the political allegory becomes clear. Shiva, like the god, will become the man of action, riot, and war – the bully, cunning in getting to the top. Saleem's gift will be the passive intellectual's who claims the artist's powers of travelling into the minds of people. The rival traits will show in their school days. Proud of being midnight's children, the boys form a privileged gang. Saleem sees the gang as a gathering of equals in which every one has the right to his own voice. Shiva, brought up on the streets and refusing to be a whining beggar, rejects Saleem's democratic dream:

'Yah, little rich boy: one rule. Everybody does what I say or I squeeze the shit outa them ... Rich kid, you don't know one damn thing! ... Where's the reason in starving, man? ... You got to get what you can, do what you can with it, and then you got to die.'

The effect of Indian independence on the rich family is to give them the opportunity to buy up the property of the departing British cheaply, and speculation drives Saleem's 'father' to delusion. When he ages, he shuts himself up to fret about getting the words of the Koran in the right order. Then the riots of partition begin; there is the war in Kashmir; identifying himself with mass-consciousness, Saleem declares the war occurred because he dreamed it; Gandhi is assassinated; there is the war between India and Pakistan. In Bombay, where Saleem's family have migrated to make money, the bombing smashes their houses and kills off several of them. These events are evoked in parodies of news-flashes from All India Radio. Saleem, indeed, sees himself as a private radio sending out his satirical reports; once they are issued, the narrative returns to his story. He has a strange sister – a delightfully mischievous girl, known as the Brass Monkey, whose main sport is setting fire to the family's shoes. When Saleem discovers the truth about his birth, he falls in love with her; she turns him down and becomes pious, and

Saleem henceforth believes all his failures in love are due to the sin of a metaphysical incest. The girl eventually becomes a superb cold-hearted singer and is 'the darling of the troops' in the war. Failure in sexual love haunts all the family. The more his 'parents' disappoint each other sexually, the more they apply themselves to loving each other. Saleem grows up to be something of a voyeur or vicarious lover.

In his attitude to love, Saleem is very much the ever wilful, inventive, teasing Scheherazade, prolonging the dreams of his people and puncturing them at the point of success. For example, his Aunt Pia, notorious for making emotional scenes, may be seen wantonly going through the motions of seducing Saleem – who is only ten at the time – but the act is physical charade: her extreme sexual provocation is put on as a 'scene' in which she rids herself of a private grief. Love is a need and custom, sexuality is play-acting. Towards the end of the book, Saleem will refuse to consummate his marriage to the witch Parvati (who has saved his life and who loves him), but not because she is pregnant by another man – in fact, his brother and opposite, the womanising Shiva. Saleem pretends he is impotent. Why this self-love? Is it possible that – too entranced by his fantastic powers of invention – he is the artist in love with storytelling itself? Or do such episodes spring from a fundamental sense that India is a chaos in which no norm can be realised? What a Westerner would call Saleem's self-pity is the egoist's devious and somehow energising passivity and resignation. It is, at any rate, the obverse of Shiva's grossly self-seeking attitude to life. Shiva is not a man to spend himself in a breathless stream of words.

All this is brought to life by Rushdie's delight in ironies of detail, which is entirely beguiling, because the smallest things, comic or horrible, are made phenomenal. But when we come to the war in East Pakistan the narrative takes on a new kind of visionary power. Saleem is a soldier, and in defeat and flight he leads a tiny group of men into the jungle – see the sorcerer's prophecy! – where he sometimes calls himself 'I', sometimes 'he' or 'buddha', and maybe also Ayooba, as if desperation had become a fever that burns out his identity. The soldiers are diminished by the rain forest, which has become a phantom personage who arouses in them all the guilt they have hidden, and punishes them for the horrors they have committed.

> But one night Ayooba awoke in the dark to find the translucent figure of a peasant with a bullet-hole in his heart and a scythe in his hand staring mournfully down at him ... After this first apparition, they fell into a state of mind in which they would have believed the forest capable of anything; each night it sent them new punishments, the accusing eyes of the wives of men they had tracked down and seized, the screaming and monkey-gibbering of children left fatherless by their work – and in this first time, the time of punishment, even the impassive buddha with his citified voice was obliged to confess that he, too, had taken to waking up at night to find the forest closing in upon him like a vice, so that he felt unable to breathe.

The forest permitted a 'double-edged' nostalgia for childhood, strange visions of mothers and fathers; Ayooba, for example, sees his mother offering her breasts, when she suddenly turns into a white monkey swinging by her tail high up in a tree. Another lad hears his father telling his brother that their father had sold his soul for a loan from his landlord, who charged three hundred per cent – 'so it seemed that the magical jungle, having tormented them with their misdeeds, was leading them by the hand towards a new adulthood'. But there are worse tests to come: in a ruined temple the soldiers are deluded by lascivious dreams of houris, evoked by a statue of a savage multi-limbed Kali. The men wake up discovering the meaninglessness of life, the pointless boredom of the desire to survive.

The experience of these very ordinary men is a purgation but not a salvation. As in an opera – and perhaps that is what *Midnight's Children* really is – the next grand scene is of comic magic. The conquering armies enter Dacca, led by a vast company of ghetto minstrels, conjurors, magic men. Marching with the troops come the entertainers:

> ... There were acrobats forming human pyramids on moving carts drawn by white bullocks; there were extraordinary female contortionists who could swallow their legs up to their knees; there were jugglers

who operated outside the laws of gravity, so that they could draw oohs and aahs from the delighted crowd as they juggled with toy grenades, keeping four hundred and twenty in the air at a time ... And there was Picture Singh himself, a seven-foot giant who weighed two hundred and forty pounds and was known as the Most Charming Man In The World because of his unsurpassable skills as a snake charmer ... he strode through the happily shrieking crowds, twined from head to foot with deadly cobras, mambas and kraits, all with their poison-sacs intact ... Picture Singh, who would be the last in the line of men who have been willing to become my fathers ... and immediately behind him came Parvati-the-witch.

She was rolling her magic basket along as she marched, and – would you believe it? – eventually helped Saleem to escape by popping him into it. After her magic, the allegory: it is Shiva who seduces Parvati and deserts her, and Picture Singh who makes Saleem marry her, in the ghetto where Picture Singh draws the crowd with his snakes while Saleem, the man of conscience, shouts political propaganda. (Mr Rushdie has already told us that the magicians are all Communists of every known hue and schism.) This episode, like so many others in the book, is almost delicately touching, but, of course, there is disaster in the next act. Back in India, Saleem is a political prisoner and is forced to submit to vasectomy. The man who lied to Parvati when he said he was impotent is now truly impotent as he dictates this long story to Padma, the working girl, who has got him a job in the pickle factory. He loves inventing chutneys – they have the power of bringing back memories.

The novel is, in part, a powerful political satire in its savaging of both political and military leaders. The narrator's hatred of Mrs Gandhi – the Widow (that is to say, the guillotine) – is deep. But I think that as satire the novel is at variance with Mr Rushdie's self-absorption and his pursuit of poetic symbols: the magic basket in which one can hide secret thoughts, and so save oneself, is an example; another is 'the hole', which recurs, and suggests that we see experience falsely, because in a little over-excited peep at a time. These symbols are rather too knowing; he is playing tricks with free association. Padma, the not-so-simple factory girl to whom the ruined Saleem dictates the book, pities his wretchedness but often suggests that he is piling it on, and is suspicious of his evasiveness. So much conjuring going on in Saleem's imagination *does* bewilder us. But as a *tour de force* his fantasy is irresistible.

Antoine de Saint-Exupéry

LOST IN THE STARS

Antoine de Sainte-Exupéry belonged to the heroic age of aviation, and in *Night Flight* he created its legend. In doing this he became, very willingly, a legend himself. The life by Marcel Migeo, *Saint-Exupéry*, sets out to separate fact from fantasy and to expound his character. The author is well placed for the task. He was a friend of Saint-Exupéry from the time they did their flight training at Neudorf, near Strasbourg, two years after the First World War. The gladiatorial period of flying was over; the first dangerous attempts to civilise flying, which began with carrying the mails, were being made. Saint-Exupéry took to the air when planes were flown by compass, map, and eye, without radio; when the top speed was a hundred miles an hour and the range no more than three hundred. Engines stalled 'with a crash as of broken crockery'. Casualties were severe. When Saint-Exupéry, failing to get into the Ecole Navale, joined what became known, almost religiously, as 'the Line', a forerunner of Air France that essayed to fly mail from Toulouse to Dakar and ultimately extended its route to South America, he faced another hazard. Pilots forced down in Africa were set upon by Moorish tribes and either tortured and killed or else held for ransom. This happened so frequently that pilots hopefully preferred to take with them an interpreter instead of a mechanic. After a year of routine flying in this service, Saint-Exupéry was stationed at a lonely desert refuelling outpost that had to deal with this hazard, and for this reason the French were later on to compare him with T. E. Lawrence.

What sort of a man was Saint-Exupéry? The first legend to go in M. Migeo's book is that he was one of the great pilots and a man for whom flying was a vocation. It is an illusion easily brought about by the overtones of mission and dedication in *Night Flight* and *Flight to Arras*. He

[123]

was, this experienced friend says, an adroit pilot but too absent-minded and eccentric to be great. He had no sense of time. He was careless. Once he left the door of his plane open and it was torn off by the wind. His attempts at long-distance records, like his flight from Paris to Saigon or from New York to Patagonia, were badly prepared and disastrous. In the cockpit his mind wandered. He was, before anything else, a writer, and he sought in flying a liberation from the boredom of city life and its worries (he was always in debt and entangled with women), as well as a spiritual liberation.

Saint-Exupéry was a very tall and eventually rather hulking man, and very plain, with a small, round head, a comically tipped-up nose, and a fixed, upward look to his eyes. (At school they called him Pique-la-Lune.) He came of a poor but aristocratic family. His father died when Saint-Exupéry was a child, and he became its dominant, restless, quarrelling, and cajoling leader, full of ideas and conversation. There is nothing, M. Migeo says, in the legend of early struggle and hardship. There were distinguished relatives to help him. He wheedled money out of his gifted mother for years. He liked to live in style. He was a gourmet. Some of his flying friends thought him a snob in the early days; if he was, snobbery was knocked out of him when he went to work for 'the Line', because men of all classes had to knuckle under to the hard work and severe discipline of that organisation. His greatest friend was a fellow-pilot, Henri Guillaumet, a peasant by origin, and a prudent, courageous, plain chap whom Saint-Exupéry pretty well worshipped. 'The Line' settled his character; his devotion to the group diminished his eccentric isolation and created in him the profound sense of the overwhelming value of duty and necessity that gives gravity to a sparkling imagination.

Saint-Exupéry's fame as a writer and his success in organising airfields in South America for his company were not of great help to him when, in the early thirties, 'the Line' was reorganised. The honeymoon with adventure was over. He entered what he called his 'blue epoch', in which he lived by journalism and film-making. His long flights failed. Saint-Exupéry the solitary lived sometimes in a blaze of publicity; occasionally he might be seen sitting at Lipp's or Les Deux Magots, pudgy and dejected, scribbling notes on bits of paper and feeling that at thirty he was finished. These notes and random articles were eventually put together, and after enormous labour they became *Wind, Sand and Stars*. This often brilliant but contrived work got the Académie award, and in America it made his fortune – a meaningless word to a man so hopelessly extravagant. Saint-Exupéry had meanwhile married a vivid, birdlike, and tempestuous Argentine widow who turned out to be a mixture of the unmanageable, the uneconomical, and (after bouts of violence) the pathetic. They frequently separated. He was a difficult man, but M. Migeo points out that this marriage at any rate satisfied the writer's need for '*inquiétude*'.

When the Second World War came, Saint-Exupéry was nearly forty. Courageously, he flew reconnaissance planes over the advancing Germans. After the fall of France, he went to New York, unluckily stopping on the way in Vichy and meeting the reputed collaborator Drieu La Rochelle. He was soon involved in those dismal slanders that affected so many Frenchmen at the time. He was at odds with de Gaulle, who he felt 'was asking the French to fight a war of fratricide', and was accused of being a Pétainiste. M. Migeo disposes convincingly of this accusation. When de Gaulle refused him any assignment during the North African campaign, he went with the American forces into Africa and, after some high-level wirepulling, was charitably allowed to fly on photographic reconnaissance over Occupied France. His eccentricities continued; many times he forgot to lower or take up his landing gear. On what was to have been his last operational flight, he disappeared. He was, it is assumed, shot down between Nice and Corsica. A German Intelligence officer who was a great admirer of him has provided evidence that his death occurred off Corsica, but M. Migeo suspects that a woman who saw two planes in combat near Nice is the true witness of his death. He was forty-four.

M. Migeo is a patient and readable biographer. He has drawn a detailed account of a brilliant, charming, ruthless egocentric who made exhausting demands on his friends, who kept them up all night while he read them his latest pages, and who was always the last customer to be tactfully edged, still talking at the top of his voice, out of *brasseries* and restaurants. Women made a set at him; he had not the art of shaking them off. M. Migeo thinks that he was not much interested in them; a writer, he was much more interested in himself. The austere, ascetic man of action, the servant of fidelity and duty, whom we picture from his writings is very different from the ebullient, self-dispensing, sensual man of real life.

When M. Migeo considers Saint-Exupéry's writings, he is less rewarding. He echoes all the contemporary praise and rejects all criticism, especially the idea that there is anything derived in his work. He makes one important but, I think, disputable reflection on *The Wisdom of the Sands*, arguing that the crucial experience of Saint-Exupéry's life was the loss of his faith in Catholicism when he was seventeen. One catches a note of regret, but the loss was permanent. Yet M. Migeo sees in Saint-Exupéry's religion of Man and his mystical humanism the line of a quest for a lost faith. I do not believe that the loss of faith had this importance. The vital event occurred, surely, much earlier, in his early boyhood: it was the death of his father. Saint-Exupéry felt deeply the need of male authority and the ruling of self and others. In *Night Flight*, Rivière, the stern builder of 'the Line', who never forgives a pilot a mistake, puts the claims of duty against the claims of love and ordinary human happiness. He is a father figure. Rivière is a portrait drawn from life, and the original saw no resemblance and did not much care for it. He was no poet and no metaphysician. He was embarrassed. Good chiefs and good pilots were not like that.

Saint-Exupéry was a poet and a man of contradictions. He was, in fact, two styles. One is plain and noble, breaking into often superb and original imagery. It is seen in *Night Flight*, in *Flight to Arras*, and in the fragments of actual experience – the crash in the desert, Madrid under bombardment – that appear in *Wind, Sand and Stars*. The other is his stained-glass-window style. Here rhetoric and mysticism conjoin. One even hears echoes of Kipling and the jingles of the Law, and one loses the traditional, singeing psychological sensibility of the French moralist. The stained-glass Saint-Exupéry is a proverb-maker writing in tiresomely archaic language (in his last book) and a conjuror of truisms. It is a curious fact that in life he was an irresistible diplomat and a mystifying adept at card tricks.

The French, when they are looking for a myth, compare Saint-Exupéry to T. E. Lawrence. As a writer, the Frenchman is by far the superior.

[126]

Both men were seized upon as possible blueprints for a contemporary hero, the technician-leader. Both were romantics. And it can be said that Saint-Exupéry got as much out of the Moroccan desert as Lawrence got out of Arabia. But Lawrence was a man of action who was able to act out his Hamlet part. He was alone. Saint-Exupéry, though he wrote much of the solitude of the airman, was not really alone. He had the group. He was – it is his favourite statement about human beings – 'a tangle of relationships'. Lawrence flattered the undisciplined instincts of his horde and their love of being hypnotised by a leader. Saint-Exupéry comes closer to the contemporary man who depends on the intricately worked-out technical order. Lawrence was conscious of guilt; one finds no trace of it in Saint-Exupéry. Both men had to consider the ineluctable, but where Lawrence, in his vanity, assumed guilty introspection, Saint-Exupéry had a far more humane insight into tragedy. But both may have been said, in Saint-Exupéry's phrase, to have 'bartered' themselves for an idea. Yet Saint-Exupéry's idea was not really to submerge himself in 'the service'. One has the impression that he was bored by it and that his mysticism was an evasion. His fundamental idea was aristocratic and French. 'What I value,' he said, 'is a certain arrangement of things. Civilisation is an invisible boon; it concerns not things we see, but the unseen bonds linking these together in one special way and not otherwise.'

Bruno Schulz

COMIC GENIUS

The ridiculous or preposterous father is a subject irresistible to the comic genius. The fellow is an involuntary god, and the variety of the species extends over the knockabout and the merely whimsical to the full wonder of incipient myth. To this last superior class the fantastic father invented by Bruno Schulz in *The Street of Crocodiles* belongs; the richness of the portrait owes everything to its brushwork and to our private knowledge that the deepest roots of the comic are poetic and even metaphysical.

Few English-speaking readers have ever heard of Schulz, and I take from his translator, Celina Wieniewska, and the thorough introduction by Jerzy Ficowski, the following notes on a very peculiar man. Schulz came of a Jewish family of dry goods merchants in the dull little town of Drogobych in Poland – it is now in the USSR – where he became a frustrated art master in the local high school and lived a solitary and hermetic life. The family's trade separated them from the ghetto; his natural language was Polish. The only outlet for his imagination seems to have been in writing letters to one or two friends, and it is out of these letters that his stories in this and other volumes grew. They were a protest against a boredom amounting to melancholia. He became famous, but found he could not live without the Drogobych he hated and he was caught there when the war began and the Nazis put him into the ghetto. It is said that a Gestapo officer who admired his drawings wangled a pass for him to leave the ghetto; one night when he took advantage of his freedom and was wandering among the crowds in the streets he was recognised and shot dead in a random shooting-up of the crowd. He was fifty years old.

It is not surprising to find comic genius of the poetic kind in serious and solitary men, but to emerge it has to feed on anomalies. We might expect – or fear – that Schulz would be a Slavonic droll in the Polish folk tradition, but he is not. Distinctly an intellectual, he translated Kafka's *The Trial* and was deep in *Joseph and His Brothers* – to my mind the most seminal of Thomas Mann's works; hence his sense of life as a collusion or conspiracy of improvised myths. Note the word 'improvised'.

Drogobych had suddenly become an American-type boom town owing to the discovery of oil, and the fantasy of Schulz takes in the shock of technology and the new cult of things and the pain of the metamorphosis. His translator is, rightly I think, less impressed by his literary sources in Kafka or surrealism than by the freedom of the painter's brush – his prose, she says, has the same freedom and originality as the brush of Chagall.

'Our Heresiarch' – as Schulz calls his secretive father, in *The Street of Crocodiles* – blossoms into speeches to his family or the seamstresses and assistants in his dress shop. He rambles into theories about the Demiurge and our enchantment with trash and inferior material. He discourses on the agonies of Matter:

> Who knows ... how many suffering, crippled, fragmentary forms of life there are, such as the artificially created life of chests and tables quickly nailed together, crucified timbers, silent martyrs to cruel human inventiveness. The terrible transplantation of incompatible and hostile races of wood, their merging into one misbegotten personality.

Misbegetting is one of his obsessions.

> Only now do I understand the lonely hero who alone had waged war against the fathomless, elemental boredom that strangled the city. Without any support, without recognition on our part, that strangest of men was defending the lost cause of poetry.

The awed seamstresses cutting out dresses to fit the draper's model in their room are told the model is alive.

Where is poetry born? In the solitary imagination of the child who instantly sees an image when he sees a thing, where the wallpaper becomes a forest, the bales of cloth turn into lakes and mountains. In this way, the father has the inventive melancholy of Quixote. The delightful

[129]

thing about him is that he is the embarrassing, scarcely visible nuisance in shop and home. It is hard to know where he is hiding or what he is up to. He is an inquiring poltergeist, coated with human modesty; even his faintly sexual ventures, like studying a seamstress's knee because he is fascinated by the structure of bones, joints, and sinews, are as modest as Uncle Toby's confusion of the fortress of Namur with his own anatomy. A minor character, like Adela the family servant, sets off the old man perfectly. She comes to clean out his room.

> He ascribed to all her functions a deeper, symbolic meaning. When, with young firm gestures, the girl pushed a long-handled broom along the floor, Father could hardly bear it. Tears would stream from his eyes, silent laughter transformed his face, and his body was shaken by spasms of delight. He was ticklish to the point of madness. It was enough for Adela to waggle her fingers at him to imitate tickling, for him to rush through all the rooms in a wild panic, banging the doors after him, to fall at last flat on the bed in the farthest room and wriggle in convulsions of laughter, imagining the tickling which he found irresistible. Because of this, Adela's power over Father was almost limitless.

This is a small matter compared with his ornithological phase when he imports the eggs of birds from all parts of the world and hatches them in the loft. The birds perched on curtains, wardrobes, lamps. (One – a sad condor – strongly resembles him.) Their plumage carpeted the floor at feeding time. The passion in due course took an 'essentially sinful and unnatural turn'.

> . . . my father arranged the marriages of birds in the attic, he sent out matchmakers, he tied up eager attractive brides in the holes and crannies under the roof, . . .

In the spring, during the migration, the house was besieged by whole flocks of cranes, pelicans, peacocks. And father himself, in an absent-minded way, would rise from the table,

> wave his arms as if they were wings, and emit a long-drawn-out bird's call while his eyes misted over. Then, rather embarrassed, he would join us in laughing it off and try to turn the whole incident into a joke.

It is a sign of Schulz's mastery of the fantastic that, at the end of the book, he has the nerve to describe how after many years the birds returned to the house – a dreadful spectacle of miscegenation, a brood of freaks, degenerate, malformed:

> Nonsensically large, stupidly developed, the birds were empty and lifeless inside. All their vitality went into their plumage, into external adornment... Some of them were flying on their backs, had heavy misshapen beaks like padlocks, were blind, or were covered with curiously coloured lumps.

In a curious passage the father compares them to an expelled tribe, preserving what they could of their soul like a legend, returning to their motherland before extinction – a possible reference to the Diaspora and the return.

Like an enquiring child, the father is wide open to belief in metamorphoses as others are prone to illness: for example he has a horror of cockroaches and, finding black spots on his skin, prepares for a tragic transformation into the creature he dreads by lying naked on the floor. But it is in the father's ornithological phase that we see the complexity of Schulz's imagination. The whole idea – it is hinted – may spring from a child's dream after looking at pictures of birds; it is given power by being planted in the father; then it becomes a grotesque nightmare; and finally we may see it as a parable, illustrating the permutations of myths which become either the inherited wastepaper of the mind or its underground. Incidentally – and how recognisable this is in childish experience – there is an overwhelming picture of the ragged idiot girl of the town sleeping on the rubbish heap, who suddenly rises from the fly-infested dump to rub herself in terrible sexual frenzy against a tree.

Under the modesty of Schulz the senses are itching in disguise. Each episode is extraordinary and carried forward fast by a highly imaged yet rational prose which is especially fine in evoking the forbidden collective wishes of the household or the town: when a comet appears in the sky and a boy comes home from school saying the end of the world is near, the whole town is enthusiastic for the end of the world. When a great gale arrives, the town becomes a saturnalia of *things* at last set free to live

[131]

as matter wants to live. There is the admonitory farce when loose-living Uncle Edward agrees to reform and to submit to the father's discovery of mesmerism and the magic of electricity. Uncle Edward is eager to shed all his characteristics and to lay bare his deepest self in the interests of Science, so that he can achieve a 'problem-free immortality'.

The dichotomy 'happy/unhappy' did not exist for him because he had been completely integrated.

Schulz's book is a masterpiece of comic writing: grave yet demented, domestically plain yet poetic, exultant and forgiving, marvellously inventive, shy and never raw. There is not a touch of whimsy in it.

Bernard Shaw

THE STAMP OF THE PURITAN

The first volume of Bernard Shaw's collected letters – there will be three more – opens in the mid-1870s when he is seen, aged eighteen, living with his drunken father and sacking himself from the job of 'accountant' – i.e., office boy – he has held for three years in Dublin, because he finds 'he has nothing to do'. This is, of course, an early Shavian gesture; really he wants to go to London.

The volume ends, 700 letters and 22 years later, when he is famous; now he is trying to rescue an actress from morphia and brandy, and insulting an Irish millionairess with an eye to wedlock. To give value for money and to expect money for value has the strong stamp of the Puritan which was primitively imbedded in Shaw's character, as was his horror of human stagnation and self-destructiveness. To the actress, Janet Achurch, he wrote that he had seen 'the process in my father; and I have never felt anything since. I learnt soon to laugh at it; and I have laughed at everything since. Presently, no doubt, I shall learn to laugh at you. What else can I do?' The loss of heart is the point, but Shaw's Bohemian family hardly encouraged that luxury. Someone wrote of his 'hard, clear, fleshless voice'.

His own addictions were the Irish addiction to words and the Puritan's to work. Add to his early novel-writing, his journalism, his musical and dramatic criticism, his pamphlets, his mass of plays with their enormous prefaces, his lecturing, his speechifying to the Fabians, his letters to the press, his active work as a borough councillor – add to these more than a quarter of a million letters full of zest and vitality and we see a man who is doubling his life.

He is a feverish and compulsive letter-writer. Like Dickens, he has no

[133]

sooner finished his work than he is up half the night writing letters and postcards to his professional friends and fans, until his eyes run with exhaustion. It is all business of some kind. Even his love-letters are that. He has a manic capacity for endless self-perpetuation as a public fantasy.

His work was not enough. Like many other Irishmen, he turned his ego into a profession. His habit was to carry his correspondence about in a sack wherever he went and to answer a handful of letters at a time while he was in buses, on trains, even when he went for a walk and sat down in a field. Like Dickens, he set up as tycoon and public performer, not only managing all his immense theatrical, literary and political business himself – and always the financial side of it with great acumen – but managing other people's as well. Unlike Dickens, in whom artist and tycoon were separated, Shaw is a single show always inseparably on the road.

There is scarcely a letter in this first volume that does not do a stage turn in order to get across some 'adamant' point. The Irish are almost always shy, almost always trying to conceal, and they have notoriously been apt to produce a stage personality to do so. Shaw's exhibitionism, his enormous vanity, his wild philanderings and gallantries are (as he often said, especially to his women correspondents) indications that he is heartless, cold, self-interested. That too is untrue: he was simply determined to preserve his freedom at all costs. Otherwise, how could he do his 18-hour day? The moment he lived by the underlying shyness – in his early days in London he was ashamed of his poverty and too frightened and gauche to go to a party – he would be bogged in Irish stagnation.

In the preface to one of his novels, 'Immaturity', he wrote about the weekly parties given by his London friends the Lawsons:

> I suffered such agonies of shyness that I sometimes walked up and down the Embankment for twenty minutes or more before venturing to knock at the door: indeed I should have funked it altogether, and hurried home asking myself what was the use of torturing myself when it was so easy to run away, if I had not been instinctively aware that I must never let myself off in this manner if I meant ever to do anything in the world. Few men can have suffered more than I did in my youth

from simple cowardice or been more horribly ashamed of it ... The worst of it was that when I appeared in the Lawsons' drawingroom I did not appeal to the goodnature of the company as a pardonably and even becomingly bashful novice. I had not then tuned the Shavian note to any sort of harmony; and I have no doubt the Lawsons found me discordant, crudely self-assertive, and insufferable.

He dropped the parties because it was wasteful to fail like that.

Success was everything, but it had, for this most austere and chaste of Irish Puritans, to be a 'clean' success; that is to say, what he and he alone would accept. No compromises. The absence of compromise in Shaw's career, as it is shown in his letters, is remarkable. He would, from sheer necessity, take on temporary commercial jobs – one was to obtain sites for telephone poles on commission at half a crown a time – but that was to keep his mother quiet while he wrote novels no one would publish.

When he got a foot in the door of journalism and lecturing, he slaved for next to nothing – at one time he was giving a hundred ill-paid lectures a year – and once he had decided on the then exceedingly unremunerative belief in Fabian Socialism, he stuck to it ruthlessly: 'If ... a man is to attain consciousness of himself as a vessel of the Zeitgeist or will or whatever it may be, he must pay the price of turning his back on the loaves and fishes, the duties, the ready-made logic, the systems and the creeds. He must do what he likes instead of doing what, on secondhand principles, he ought.'

On secondhand principles, he goes on, he ought to have got a safe job to save his dear old mother from living on a second floor and teaching schoolgirls to sing. He refused, and what is the result? '... my mother, the victim of my selfishness, is a hearty, independent and jolly person, instead of a miserable old woman dragged at the chariot wheels of her miserable son, who had dutifully sacrificed himself for her comfort.'

This is well-known Shavian stuff: Shaw's Socialism got a strong boost from his dislike of family strangulation. The theory of the pursuing female evidently arises, as the letters show, because he was much pursued, philandered to escape and, if caught, refers (with an eighteenth-century gallantry) to the lady as his 'seductress'. (He was, as all the Anglo–Irish were, a throwback to the eighteenth century.) He often remarks that his Irish gallantry to women takes the English aback: it does. It indicates mystification rather than performance.

Shaw falls back on the idea that women rarely love – which his one or two complete love affairs violently contradict – but, rather, affectionately pity men for falling in love with them, and treat them like babies. This argument was hopelessly out of date in Victorian times and prepares the way for the enslaving of women.

So, shifting his ground again, Shaw takes the genial line with actress after actress, to the woman who became his wife, that he is going to get what he can out of them and throw them aside; and that they will benefit by having worked with him! This was, of course, the rude-shy approach. A letter to his future wife, who had invited him to go on holiday to Dieppe, at a moment when 'the sprite', as Beatrice Webb called him, was worn out with overwork – and really scared – illustrates the point:

> I am to embark in a piercing wind, with lifeboats capsizing and ships foundering in all directions; to go to a watering place in the depth of winter with nothing to do and nowhere to go; I am to be chaperoned by two women, each determined that the other shall seduce me and each determined that I shall not seduce her . . .
>
> No use in looking for human sympathy from me. I have turned the switch, and am your very good friend, but as hard as nails.

The joke did not succeed. There are times when artificial comedy annoys. The future Mrs Shaw was as Irish and shy as he was, and he had a hard time living this letter down.

Shaw's letters are good because they are sharp, shrewd about people, comic, direct, always good-natured, contain news and have a core of purpose. He is the plausible speaker convincing an audience, and that core of seriousness is flattering. His letters are as lively when he is writing to the Webbs and the other Fabians as when he writes to his theatrical and literary correspondents. Shaw says in one of them that as a writer he sees life less as people than as fragments of situation. For this reason alone he was a born playwright, and it is odd that a man as experienced in the theatre as William Archer was should not have spotted it; but Archer was stuffy.

There is a situation in every letter; and in spite of what he says, a very subtle sense of character and its relation to the possible actor or actress, in his plays. The letters of outright criticism or advice to famous people like Ellen Terry or Mrs Patrick Campbell are incisive. The letter to Charrington, Janet Achurch's husband, tactfully suggesting that he is unsuitable for the part of Morrell in *Candida*, is a masterpiece.

There is always the tenderness of play in the letters to Ellen Terry (the next volume, I presume, will contain the bulk of them), but in the letters to Janet Achurch there is more than tenderness: there is a deep concern, an expression of the humanity and seriousness that Shaw would sometimes allow to come out; in her case because she has come so wretchedly close to his own, never-forgotten, wretched home background.

The glimpses of a concealed inner Shaw are rare – some lines in the long correspondence with Janet Achurch, the Ibsen actress, a very old friend, are among the few instances. They contain a glimpse of the inciting misery, shame, loneliness and frustration of his early Dublin life, and then quickly the shutter closes with the laugh that enables him to escape onto the stage.

An early boyish letter to his sister Lucinda, the singer, shows him preternaturally sagacious and ruthless for his years: '. . . you have only to be immoveable, polite, generally amicable, and adamant . . .' 'You ought to laugh at Mamma more than you do.' That is the Shavian essence: Stand on your own, laugh at everyone but heal the wound by the skill of your laughter. Shaw enraged, yet he never made an enemy. Perhaps because he went beyond enraging into the fantasy world of outrage.

One long grave letter takes Janet Achurch, as it were, aside, and talks privately to her, quietly turning over the case for the advantages and disadvantages of religion. In its real sense – the Puritan argues – it is re-creation, the remaking of the self; it can arise from formal religion, from love, from art. We must have recreation or else stimulation. 'The question is, how am I to make Janet religious, so that she may recreate herself and feel no need of stimulants. That is the question that obsesses me.'

It did obsess him, and people have often wondered at it. The fact is that, in another way, his own case was like hers. His addiction was to words and his cleverness with them; but like her, he depended on an audience and knew the price this exacted. I am not sure that he was a great letter-writer; but his letters must have been delightful to receive; unlike Voltaire, who was called a chaos of clear ideas, he was a chaos of clear arguments. They become monotonous, and in letters his predictability shows up. Strangely, it is not the performer who dazzles here, for he repeats his tricks. The happy shock of the unfair argument wears off.

What really gets us is that the performer is at heart the industrious apprentice – one whom we indeed see at the end of this volume winning the great gamble and about to marry the capitalist boss's daughter. It is a moral story.

John Updike

GETTING RICHER

The key to John Updike's 'Rabbit' novels is in the last phrase of this opening passage from *Rabbit Is Rich*:

> Running out of gas, Rabbit Angstrom thinks as he stands behind the summer-dusty windows of the Springer Motors display room watching the traffic go by on Route 111, traffic somehow thin and scared compared to what it used to be. The fucking world is running out of gas. But they won't catch him, not yet, because there isn't a piece of junk on the road gets better mileage than his Toyotas, with lower service costs. Read *Consumer Reports*, April issue. That's all he has to tell the people when they come in. And come in they do, the people out there are getting frantic, they know the great American ride is ending.

We don't suppose Rabbit is all that rich – not as rich as the old Pennsylvania mineowners were – but as a lower-middle-class citizen of the shrewd kind he has done pretty well, marrying the boss's daughter, in the manner of the industrious apprentice. In a beautiful scene of furtive comedy, we see him buying Krugerrands. Still, there is alarm in that last phrase of his. It contains something like a metaphysical message. Huck Finn's classic American dream of 'lighting out for the territory' – into whatever wilderness of contemporary *moeurs*, or even of the spirit, one likes to think of is done for. That 'ride' as pure escape sets the pace in the first of the 'Rabbit' novels, when Harry Angstrom swung impulsively on to the highway, heading south, away from Janice, his tippling, muddling 'mutt' of a wife. He is dragged back by news of tragedy at home: befuddled, she had drowned her baby, as we read in Updike's carefully documented account of the awful physical conditions of the case. If Rabbit was guilty by association, he had at any rate left her a car, that secondary sexual organ of our contemporary life. In *Rabbit Redux*, he was reduced to guilty matrimony, and it was Janice who lit out – with Stavros, her father's Greek assistant – and with even more appalling results. That volume seems to me the most impressive of the chronicle: it had Thomas Hardy-like items in it. In the present one, it is Rabbit's son who lights out – of college, to accuse the forty-six-year-old father he loves and hates. Here Updike's difficulty is to find a means of insinuating the sins of the past without recapitulating them and to make the novel something more than a job of clearing up. All his astonishing technical virtuosity as a poet, chronicler, moralist, and storyteller is called for. I detect some change of tone, but he has at any rate escaped the journalistic telegraphese that ruined, say, the later 'Forsyte' and other sagas. And if *Rabbit Is Rich* is in danger of becoming an essay in latter-day Babbittry, the author does fill out a man ashamed of his shamelessness; Rabbit is shown puzzled by his inescapable Puritan guilts, and relieved by bursts of rancour. As a one-time basketball hero, he has not much more in his head than the ethos of the 'achiever': you must 'win'. Beyond that, he is so cloudy in mind that he never really knows whether, morally speaking, he is lighting out or lighting back. Some critics have called him a monster, but he is far from that. Even in his tiresome sexual obsession he is excusable, having come to sex later than the young do today. He is really a deedy infant, and moderately decent: he'd like to learn. If he doesn't quite know how to love his wife, he is sentimentally protective; in the common love–hate between father and son, he is honest, though his methods are risky. The son swings between thinking of his father as a murderer of a baby and a wacky girl (but by default) and thinking of him as a comforting shadow. The curse of the cult of 'achievement' has its misleading aspects.

If we look first of all at Updike as a chronicler, we have to say that he was dead right in choosing the minor provincial city of Brewer, Pennsylvania, and putting Rabbit into the motor trade. That trade is the source of inner-city decay. This kind of ad hoc city has become international; horrible world news pours in via 'the boob tube', and adds new fantasies to what one has to call the 'ongoing' private stream of domestic consciousness – one recalls that in Joyce, to whom Updike has a debt, that stream mainly flowed back. The next element is native American, even though it has spread: television's real contribution to the mind comes from the Things in the commercials, with their awful jollities. Updike has the extraordinary gift of making the paraphernalia of, say, the Sears Roebuck catalogue sound like a chant from the Book of Psalms turned into vaudeville. Industrialised society consumes and worships what can be bought. As Henry James once told us, 'the shopping' is in the blood. Updike knows, for example, every gadget in a car, from the engine to the coachwork, even to the point of giving us the useful information that it is not easy to perform the act of lust on vinyl seating.

It has always seemed to me that in his preoccupation with the stillness of domestic objects Updike is a descendant, in writing, of the Dutch genre painters, to whom everything in a house, in nature, or in human posture had the gleam of usage on it without which a deeply domestic culture could not survive its own boredom. The stress on paraphernalia, even the label on the product, has put something vivid into American comic writers as well as serious moralists. By extension, the clothes and under-clothes of people, the parts of their bodies – heads, faces, ears, noses, legs, arms, hands, toes, complexions, and the hungrier organs – are minutely noted. (Rabbit's son is upset because his wife has one nostril larger than the other.) I don't mean that these things are catalogued by Updike; they simply give the ripple of ballad-like vividness to the stream of consciousness. If downtown Brewer looks as if it had been bombed by its loving inhabitants, Updike is as exact as a war artist who rises far above the documentary and the unfelt. Like Eliot, he is moved by the waste land. Where Sinclair Lewis's clutter of mind and matter pushed at us the brutalised pathos of accepted vulgarities, Updike is a poet. He loves words and images. If his sexual curiosity runs to the clinical, he relieves us with gnomic sentences; perhaps the closeups of sex, the private porn, are 'a kind of penance at your root'. There is a preacher inside him who says that if 'anything goes', there is a price, which, for some unfair reason, a Mediterranean like Stavros never has to pay; unlike the Puritan Rabbit, and knowing he will die, Stavros has a 'superior grip upon the basic elements of life'. If he is compelled in his pursuit of pleasure, he knows how to give it; in bed, he loves a distracting chat and the small talk of the affections, the fun of taking sex as friendship, not a climax. He has the old Greek sense that 'nothing too much' lasts longest. This is what charms Rabbit's wife.

One sees the ex-athlete Rabbit closer to his particular norm as he takes up jogging when that absurd craze comes to the health-clowns of Brewer. Updike is the poet of physical action:

> [Rabbit] begins to run. In the woods, along the old logging roads and bridle trails, he ponderously speeds in tennis shoes first, orange with clay dust, and then in gold-and-blue Nikes bought at a sporting goods shop in Stroudsburg especially for this, running shoes with tipped-up soles at toe and heel, soles whose resilient circlets like flattened cleats lift him powerfully as, growing lighter and quicker and quieter, he runs.

The one-time athletic Puritan is all conscious of the 'murderous burden swaddled about his heart and lungs' in the early days of these desperate bids for immortality. He experiences fanaticism about his body but eventually finds himself 'casting his mind wide' and becomes aware of the country, and, indeed, more:

> There is along the way an open space, once a meadow, now spiked with cedars and tassle-headed weeds, where swallows dip and careen, snapping up insects revived in the evening damp. Like these swallows Rabbit, the blue and gold of his new shoes flickering, skims, above the earth, above the dead. The dead stare upwards. Mom and Pop are lying together again as for so many years on that sway-backed bed they'd bought second-hand during the Depression and never got around to replacing though it squeaked like a tricycle left out in the rain and was so short Pop's feet stuck out of the covers. Papery-white feet that got mottled and marbled with veins finally: if he'd ever have exercised he might have lived longer. Tothero [the sports coach] down there is all eyes, eyes big as saucers staring out of his lopsided head while his swollen tongue hunts for a word. Fred Springer, who put Harry where he is, eggs him on, hunched over and grimacing like a man with a

[142]

poker hand so good it hurts. Skeeter, that that newspaper clipping claimed had fired upon the Philly cops first even though there were twenty of them in the yard and hallways and only some pregnant mothers and children on the commune premises, Skeeter black as the earth turns his face away.

(Skeeter we remember as the mixture of Negro religion and conspiracy, on the run in *Rabbit Redux* – the one profoundly tragic character in that book.)

Rabbit is running silent as an Indian when he gets into the pine needles of the woods:

Becky [his drowned baby], a mere seed laid to rest, and Jill [burned to death in a fire], a pale seedling held from the sun, hang in the earth, he imagines, like stars, and beyond them there are myriads, whole races like the Cambodians, that have drifted into death. He is treading on them all, they are resilient, they are cheering him on, his lungs are burning, his heart hurts, he is a membrane removed from the hosts below, their filaments caress his ankles, he loves the earth, he will never die.

He gets home, and his wife says, 'For heaven's sakes. What are you training for?' He says the thing is to press against your limitations. 'It's now or never ... There's people out to get me. I can lie down now. Or fight.' And when she asks who is trying to get him, he says, 'You should know' – it's that damn son of theirs. 'You hatched him.' She is an incompetent woman, who can't shop, cook, or keep a house even fairly clean, and he does not know whether he loves her or not, but he'll never leave her. I quote these long passages because they are examples of Updike's mastery of allusive narrative, which mingles past guilts and mistakes with the going world of the present.

In this volume, we realise that the women, even when they are victims, are stronger than Rabbit is, for a reason he somehow stumbles on. Men are solitaries and egotists; foolish or not, they see themselves as born to be alone. The women are not solitaries. Their strength lies in their capacity for assimilating personal relationships, in living for the primacy of family and accepting its hierarchies. Rabbit may earn the money, out of compulsion; the women control the capital, real or emotional. They live by arrangements among themselves and never forget a nourishing jealousy.

The two earlier novels had a tight, dramatic tension. In the present one, the tension is looser, because the elders are getting fat and middle-aged, but there is the new drama of the puzzled father and the son who too much resembles him. The 'four o'clock garbage' of television still filters in from the outside world. There is comedy: the scene with the 'broad-minded' young minister who is called in to marry the unbelieving young people in church. The son is ashamed among his shacking-up friends, who are often high on pot or beer, for weakly marrying a girl merely because she is pregnant by him. Worse, she is not a student from the college he has dropped out of but is a mere secretary – loss of group caste there. But she is strong enough to call her young macho a 'twerp', to have her baby, and to let her husband go back to college. He makes the startling discovery that since she has been obliged to cut education and to work for a living, she is more grown up, more independent than his student friends. Among the young women, she is the fullest and most subtle portrait in the novel.

Janice, Rabbit's wife, in her devious way, grows stronger the more muddled she is. And, of course, Grandmother Springer, with her split-minded sentences, is the confident voice of Fate itself. But the clinching final incident is Rabbit's sentimental journey to see Ruth, the wronged woman of *Rabbit, Run*. She belongs, in the American class system, to the stoical, rural, hard-tongued poor. Rabbit burns to know, in his shame-faced sexy way, whether she bore him a daughter or whether she had an abortion. He hints at putting his hand in his pocket. With the mastery of the Sphinx, she evades telling him. Or, indeed, us. This scene has the wit of a Molière comedy. She tells him, quietly, that her dead husband was the best father her children could have had and more of a man than Rabbit could hope to be. She had been a used woman, but she had known, in her grim way, how to become unused. In the meantime, the middle-aged friends of Rabbit have drifted into the pricey hedonism of trying to copy the young. They drink rather too much. There is a muddled wife-swapping holiday for these 'oldies' in the Caribbean in which the women put their heads together and see that Rabbit, especially, does not get the partner he had hoped for. After this, the porn magazines lose their spell; the elders return making moral grimaces. A phrase about shadows falling – they 'sneak in like burglars' – evokes the emotional experience of so many of the inhabitants of Brewer.

There is nothing in this volume as searing as the Skeeter episode in *Rabbit Redux*, but that in fact enhances the conviction that these three books of Updike's are a monumental portrayal of provincial and domestic manners. He is both poet and historian, so various in observation and so truthful, so inventive and adept, that he leaves us brooding on his scene and remembering his epithets.

Rebecca West

─────

She 'lived her life operatically and tinkered endlessly with the story-line, the score and the libretto'. These frank words come from Victoria Glendinning's sympathetic and searching life of Cicily Fairfield, known to us as Rebecca West. Operatic? The mind wanders to the stormy life of George Sand, who had also been a combative journalist and a richly textured novelist reckless in her passions, and of whom her daughter wrote, 'It will take a clever fellow to unravel the character of my mother.' It would appear that Rebecca West felt in her old age that the story of her life required two clever fellows. In Ms Glendinning's introduction we read that Rebecca West left 'a signed request' that Ms Glendinning, who had known her well during the last ten years of her life, should write a short biography while we were waiting for a fuller life by Stanley Olson. The choice was happy. Ms Glendinning is a well-known, prize-winning biographer of such difficult ladies as Edith Sitwell and Vita Sackville-West and of the admirable Elizabeth Bowen. In this last, she seemed somewhat nervous of that electric Anglo–Irish brain, but with Rebecca West she is alert to the pathos, the grand drama of sweeping judgement. She understands how the tunes of temperament change.

Why did the young Miss Fairfield choose to be Rebecca West? (She disliked Ibsen's plays.) To re-imagine herself? To catch attention? To stand apart from her sisters, one of whom was already making an impression as a distinguished doctor and would eventually become a barrister, while the other sister was blamelessly conventional? We must look back to Rebecca's Puritan Scottish mother, of crofter stock, and her fantasising Anglo–Irish father. The parents met in Australia, where they were poor immigrants. He had become a painter and a clever, restless journalist, inclined to parlous mining speculations and casual love affairs. The marriage was a union of two lonely people. Hating Australia, he brought her back to Scotland. No Puritan he. He came from wild Kerry, and his fancy was filled with talk of rank and with Anglo–Irish obsession with grand cousinage. The daughters listened in their childhood to his tales of an ancestor who had been a cousin of Sir Walter Raleigh, of a connection with the great Sackvilles which somehow gave them all descent from an aunt of Anne Boleyn. Even Rebecca's older and sterner sister, Lettie, the distinguished doctor, when she turned Roman Catholic spoke of the family connection with a procession of saints – St Margaret of Scotland, St Louis of France, two Russian saints, and a Spanish one.

More interesting was the father's political talk. He was an admirer of Edmund Burke and corresponded with Herbert Spencer. When he brought his family back to Scotland, he worked in Glasgow on the *Glasgow Herald*, and then moved them to London. Eventually, he vanished abroad on some speculative pharmaceutical deal, pursued women, and abandoned the family completely for five years – it is possible that his wife threw him out – and was found dead in lodgings in Liverpool. In the meantime, the mother raised the family in Edinburgh. Her gift was musical, and her taste for Schumann and the influence of music in general were to be strong in Rebecca's writing. In Edinburgh, the Athens of the North, the clever girls soon won scholarships to excellent schools. Rebecca's desire was to become an actress, and when she was seventeen she went to London to the Academy of Dramatic Art. There, for all her gifts and although she did get one or two minor parts, she failed. Why? The beautiful girl was histrionic. The victim of high-strung nervousness, she reacted to strain with involuntary grimaces and was plagued by uncontrollable itchings. In short, she could not unself herself and become other people.

She inherited from her father a literary gift, but it would have startled him to see her succeed as an ardent feminist. He had been a strong Tory, and loathed the notion of women's suffrage: suffragettes, he said, were 'unsympathetic and repellent'. He would have been shocked by the articles she wrote for *The Freewoman*, though he certainly would have admired her mastery of the irreverent metaphor, which caught the attention of

Bernard Shaw. We hear her dismissing the British intelligentsia as 'the left-wing carriage trade'. (Much later in her life, at the time of the abdication of Edward VIII, she was to write of the King that his mind seemed to be like 'a telephone exchange with not enough subscribers'.) Such wit in her writing and conversation led the young woman to the famous, but it had its price. One of her lifelong friends, the distinguished journalist Charles Curran, who was of great help to her when she was writing her long, incisive investigative studies of crime and treachery, said of her that she 'has several skins fewer than any other human being, it's a kind of psychological haemophilia, which is one reason why she writes so well, and why she is so vulnerable'.

Vulnerable especially in love, as we see in the notorious and painful affair with H. G. Wells. How could she have ignored the warnings of his disastrous public affair with the young Amber Reeves? How could the young Rebecca not perceive or understand Wells's gratitude to his wife? Rebecca's headlong ambition in love led to neurotic illness, and this was to be repeated in her love affair with Beaverbrook, the newspaper tycoon. The extravagance of feeling was certainly operatic in the sense that it was orchestrated and, in fact, led to disturbing, and even fantastic, illusions.

The young woman, who had been a 'displaced person' as a child, not unnaturally sought the glamour of wealth and respectable certainty. We come at last to her marriage with Henry Andrews, notoriously a pedant, apparently rich, and a bore. He passed as a solid English country gentle-man, but he, too, had been a displaced person. He came of Polish or Lithuanian stock, had been educated in Great Britain, and had spent several years in a prison camp in Germany during the First World War. He dabbled in merchant banking, not always happily: he was really by nature a fussing academic. (When he and Rebecca set up in a rather grand country house in Buckinghamshire, the local villagers were mystified by him and lightly called him 'a comical old bugger'.) For Rebecca, he had one valuable gift: he was a linguist. This was indispensable to her on her visits to Yugoslavia before 1939, when she wrote what is thought by many to be a masterpiece of romantic travel, *Black Lamb and Grey Falcon*. As her biographer says, Rebecca became 'one of nature's Balkans', and, indeed, at one point in *Black Lamb and Grey Falcon* her chatty husband is heard saying to her, 'As for your other demands that from now on every day will be an apocalyptic revelation, I should drop that, if I were you!' But she didn't. John Gunther, her great friend, said the book was not so much about Yugoslavia as about Rebecca West. She herself wrote in a well-known passage:

> Only part of us is sane: only part of us loves pleasure and the longer day of happiness, wants to live to our nineties and die in peace, in a house that we built, that shall shelter those who come after us. The other half of us is nearly mad.... [This fight] can be observed constantly in our personal lives.

True or untrue, the overtone is operatic: even the scenery, the archaeology, the history, and many of the people seem to be stage chorus.

Ms Glendinning has made much of Rebecca West's admiration for Proust and the music of his long-winded and branching sentences, and of his influence on her. This is true up to a point; in her novels (except in *The Fountain Overflows*) we often have the sensation of claustrophobia. Wells complained that in the narrative of her early novel *The Judge* she was dilatory and began too far back. This is also true of her last novel, *The Birds Fall Down* – an ambitious historical story in which an innocent girl is used to carry a message to czarist dissidents. We are soon lost in the décor and the overfurnishing of the intrigue. Too many people appear, too completely. The whole story is too brilliantly laboured. It is astonishing that while she was working on this very long book the manic side of her temperament was driving her to write scores of letters to friends, explaining here, attacking there, as she poured out the wrongs of her personal life: the tedium of her marriage; the persisting quarrel with her son, Anthony; her feuds with her critics, who rightly accused her of political extremism. Her health was bad. After a serious operation, she had hallucinations: she said that the wretched Henry Andrews was trying to poison her with doctored soup sent over from a London restaurant.

In 1968, Henry died. His organised fussiness was revealed. In the waistcoat pockets of thirty Savile Row suits – all the suits the same – a hundred and eighty-seven pounds was found: money the prudent man had reserved for tips! A more disturbing discovery was that he had been in the habit of casually picking up girls. Rebecca was enraged. She had only briefly been unfaithful to him – once with a doctor and once in Nuremberg, with a judge at the trial. In itself rather an odd choice.

Rebecca West lived on until she was ninety. She sold the Buckingham-shire mansion and moved to a terrace in Kensington, a few doors from the Iranian Embassy that later sheltered terrorists. A highly trained anti-terrorist squad attacked the building, and she eagerly watched the affair from her window until she was dramatically rescued in a scene of gunfire. The incident is an ironic and unexpected crown of her career. She could almost have invented it.

Oscar Wilde

AN ANGLO—IRISHMAN

The late Richard Ellmann's *Oscar Wilde* runs to nearly 600 pages, is exhaustive but not in the leaden manner of the fact-fetishist, but in the humane spirit of fervent enquiry. In Wilde he has an Anglo–Irishman who acts his reckless way through the hidden intimacies of late Victorian society, a man brimming with wit, images and inventive afterthoughts in his progress to fame and his own undoing. When reporters crowded round Wilde on his arrival on his first trip to New York and asked the dandy what impression the stormy Atlantic ocean had made upon him, Wilde replied that it seemed tame to him. The reporters cabled to London: 'Mr Wilde Disappointed with the Atlantic'; but Ellmann reminds us that Wilde had once denounced the sea as being 'unvintageable'. He was a man who could always outdo himself. Yet Mr Ellmann shows, Wilde is also the classic tragic hero, self-destroyed at the height of his fame, 'refulgent, proud and ready to fall'. The fall is dreadful but it is perfect that it begins when the greatest of his comedies, *The Importance of Being Earnest*, is entrancing London audiences and masks his own secret life as a homosexual. It is perfect also that when Wilde returns one night to his club he finds a card from the Marquess of Queensberry containing the fatal ill-spelt words: 'To Oscar Wilde, posing Somdomite' – a blow below the belt from the author of the world-famous Queensberry rules for boxers, also the father – himself a minor poet – who is determined to rescue his son, Lord Alfred Douglas, from Wilde's love and influence. Wilde loses his head, brings an action for libel against the rough and noble fox-hunter and in the following trials Wilde is at the mercy of deadlier actors than himself: the lawyers. They have collected evidence from male prostitutes and in the trial that follows for 'indecent behaviour'

Wilde is done for. Almost two generations will pass before that particular law, now known as the 'blackmailer's charter', is repealed.

Wilde's father was a fashionable and distinguished Dublin eye surgeon and had been knighted: he founded St Mark's Hospital in Dublin for special treatment of the eye and ear. He was also a scholarly authority on the neglected, pre-historic Barrows of Ireland and an outstanding expert on Irish folklore. A scholar, he was no saint: he had fathered three illegitimate children before his marriage and his wife was far too proud or indifferent to complain. She was an Irish patriot, she stood for Irish freedom and was also a poetess who felt herself 'destined for greatness'. She claimed to have been an eagle in an earlier life on earth; that her family, the Elgees, were of Italian origin, called herself Speranza and was as famous for her flamboyant clothes as her son was for his. When Oscar was born in 1854 she gave him operatic names – Oscar Fingal O'Flahertie Wills Wilde – the O'Flahertie in honour of her supposed family connection with pre-Norman Kings of West Connacht who had provoked the famous Galway prayer 'From the wild O'Flaherties good Lord deliver us'. Convinced of the genius of her son she saw to it that he was sent to a school known as the 'Irish Eton' near Enniskillen, then on to Trinity, Dublin, where he became an excellent classicist. The youth was already an aesthete. He went on to Magdalen, Oxford, where despite some delinquencies, he triumphed by winning the Newdigate Prize for poetry and indeed got a Double First.

Mr Ellmann writes:

> And so Wilde created himself at Oxford. He began by stirring his conscience with Ruskin and his senses with Pater; these worthies gradually passed into more complicated blends of Catholicism, Freemasonry, aestheticism . . . Initially he tried to resolve his own contradictions. But gradually . . . he came to see his contradictions as a source of strength rather than of volatility.

He will have the art of becoming other people.

At Oxford he lost, or was careful to lose, his Irish accent. On his successful lecture tours in America the actor in him brought it back when he left the East and faced the descendants of the poor Irish emigrants.

They were not much interested in the pre-Raphaelitism or the House Beautiful, or even his socialism. For them he became the poetic Speranza's son, the Irish patriot. One had supposed that his extraordinary clothes – the romantic cloak, the extravagantly wide collar, the velvet knickerbockers and the silk stockings – not to mention the touches of jewellery – that his tall massive figure would draw ridicule. Far from it. Americans delighted in fantastic clothes in their parades. Wilde's costume was not an eccentricity: he was more than half an actor and he was also protesting against the heavy frock coat of conventional Puritan success. Still, he was not a man to be taken by surprise. Hearing that some students intended to jeer, he adroitly appeared in conventional dinner-jacket. The revolt was killed. In his private meetings with famous American writers Longfellow and, above all, Whitman were impressed. Only Henry James – who was to have his own secret – felt there was something 'unclean' in him.

We come to Wilde's return to Great Britain and his marriage to Constance Lloyd. It seems certain that he had had homosexual contacts in Oxford where they were tolerated and even fashionable. Ellmann says that Wilde had caught syphilis there and thinks that the marriage to Constance could have been long delayed on this account. The courtship of Constance was indeed slow. Her mother had died, her father had remarried and the girl lived with her grandfather, a lawyer. She was shy and said by Ellmann to be 'logical, mathematical, shy yet fond of talking', could read Dante in Italian – '(and did)'. There are touching lines in a letter she wrote to her future husband about the failure of his early play *Vera* in America. She says, with a ring of truth, about her life:

> The world surely is unjust and bitter to most of us; . . . There is not the slightest use in *fighting* against existing prejudices . . . I am afraid you and I disagree in our opinions on art, for I hold that there is no perfect art without perfect morality, whilst you say that they are distinct and separable things. . . . Truly I am no judge that you should appeal to me for opinions.

She was (as Ellmann says) 'intelligent, . . . capable and independent'. She was certainly well-read in French and Italian literature and 'learned German so they could enjoy reading new books in the language together'.

[153]

When at last they married they moved into 'the House Beautiful' Wilde had planned and which is described in detail. We note that the library where he worked had pale gold walls and that 'along two sides of the room was a low divan, in front of which were ottomans, lanterns, and hangings, an Eastern inlaid table and – no chairs.' And in one of the drawing rooms upstairs, appropriately, a small bronze figure of Narcissus. Wilde was indeed in love with himself and 'played the married man with a flair which suggested that for him it was an adventure rather than a quiescence'. Even more a dangerous display of the double nature of the born wit.

The sudden success in the theatre with *Lady Windermere's Fan* and *A Woman of No Importance* splits his emotional, social and sexual life. The homosexuality which had been stirred at tolerant Oxford puts him at the mercy of the young Alfred Douglas and, as Ellmann says, if Wilde was bold, Douglas was totally reckless – 'reckless and unmanageable ... Since neither Wilde nor Douglas practiced or expected sexual fidelity, money was the stamp and seal of their love.' And 'like a figure in Greek tragedy, Wilde had allowed his success to make him overweening'. And Douglas was a young man who, like his father, thrived on quarrels. As we follow the detail the sole comfort in a tangled story is Wilde's generosity to the spendthrift young man who is destroying him.

What we have forgotten is that there were three trials: Wilde's defiance of Queensberry failed. Wilde's wife and friends urged him to go to France. He refused to take his chance. Boy prostitutes saw immense prospects of blackmail and he was easily trapped.

Ellmann writes:

A half-packed suitcase lay on the bed, emblem of contradictory impulses. He was tired of action. Like Hamlet, as he understood that hero, he wished to distance himself from his plight, to be the spectator of his own tragedy ... He had always met adversity head on ... It was like the history of Timon of Athens or of Wilde's old admiration, Agamemnon, yet meaner.

In London his two plays *An Ideal Husband* and *The Importance of Being Earnest* were taken off. The same happened in New York. At the second trial the jury disagreed. At the third trial he was done for.

We know the rest. In Reading Gaol the Governor ruled by the book and it was a long time before Wilde was permitted to read anything. Later conditions were a little easier and his warders were distinctly sympathetic. *The Ballad of Reading Gaol* tells his story. We may have become dubious of the famous line 'Each man kills the thing he loves' as a tragic utterance but the portraits of his awed fellow-prisoners are not easily forgotten. His life in France after his release is a life without a role. We see him uncertain and dismayed, when, by accident, some old acquaintance hesitates to recognise him; he can only beg with his eyes or turn away. In the final scene in the little hotel in Paris the proprietor is decent but the death of Wilde is horrible. He is living on lethal draughts of absinthe and brandy and dies horribly of syphilis. (His body burst.) He was buried in the cemetery of Bagneux. In 1909 the body was moved to Père Lachaise and has Epstein's famous monument and lines from *The Ballad of Reading Gaol*:

> And alien tears will fill for him
>   Pity's long-broken urn,
> For his mourners will be outcast men,
>   And outcasts always mourn.

He belongs to our world, Ellmann says, more than to Victoria's: I am not sure what that sentence means unless it is that we share in the general vengeance of the gods?

P. G. Wodehouse

NEVER-NEVER-LAND

Among the writers who are celebrating the centenary of the birth of P. G. Wodehouse this year, Benny Green seems to me the most spirited and cogent to have appeared so far. He calls his book 'a *literary* biography' (my italics), which is exactly what is called for in dealing with a surprisingly scholarly master of comic folly, who in spite of poor eyesight seems to have done nothing but write all day, almost from the cradle until his ninetieth year. If he had another secret life behind his writing he was preoccupied enough to make it impenetrable. He was clearly a professional but one with the gift of imperturbable and deedy innocence.

He remained a schoolboy for life but without the sentimental morbidities of, say, Barrie or Milne's tinklings from the kindergarten. If he has a literary coeval, this is 'perhaps' – as Mr Green says – the Max Beerbohm of *Zuleika Dobson*. Not perhaps at all: this is real insight. Wodehouse was certainly an Edwardian and much influenced by the D'Oyly Carte opera, and one recalls that the age was remarkable for producing a number of comic writers of ingrained 'English light humour'; like a dry white wine it nourished the assumptions, malice, and comforts of F. Anstey, Saki, one book of Jerome K. Jerome's, the Grossmiths, and W. W. Jacobs. They were 'English' in the very sap of that conceit: they travelled well in America in their time, especially Wodehouse himself, though I have found lately that flocks of American students have never heard of him. This is sad but understandable. The age of lightheaded imperial innocence began to vanish after 1914 and we have grown up in the black laughter of outrage, enhanced by the obsession with sex. One can only say that laughter for its own sake is never *passé* for very long: we still laugh at Goldsmith and Restoration comedy after a spell of sneering at their subjects, their oaths and delivery.

[156]

It has been said, especially of light comedy, that its writers are apt to be trapped by period and the presumptions of its manners and vernacular; that none of us has known a butler or 'gentleman's gentleman', a rich silly-ass with a monocle, like Wooster, or a barmy peer like Lord Emsworth; that their idiotic world is dead. One has heard it scathingly argued that these fools are socially and politically deplorable, propaganda for reactionary causes and against what used to be called 'the challenge of our time'. Our nostalgia ought to be for the future. The argument is crabbed. The kingdoms of fantasy and mirth are long-lasting and not of this world; and their inhabitants make circles round our respectable angers. The strength of Wodehouse lies not in his almost incomprehensibly intricate plots – Restoration comedy again – but in his prose style and there, above all, in his command of mind-splitting metaphor. To describe a girl as 'the sand in civilisation's spinach' enlarges and decorates the imagination.

Of course the society into which Wodehouse was born in 1881 has its importance either as an influence or as a springboard. I am old enough to have known the rather rueful beginning of the end of his period and, by chance, to have lived in his sainted Dulwich, and to have been briefly educated at what was called the Lower School – lower in social class, and more productive of bank clerks than colonial governors, than was his Dulwich College, the subject, incidentally, of one of Pissarro's romantic Anglophile paintings. The 'romance' and pleasances of what was then one of the most vernal London suburbs, and the niceties of its local snobberies, are well known to me. (The College's second cricket team would condescend to play our first once a year and often beat us. They, we used to say, had expensive coaches!) We belonged to the same Elizabethan foundation, Alleyn's College of God's Gift.

I felt the Dulwich dream of the time and did not much repine because it was certain not to be realised, though we copied items of its swank. One or two of our senior boys would cause a stir by playing at being dressy Bertie Wooster and putting on a monocle to annoy the masters. (Some learned writers to the London *Times* have claimed that the monocle was added by vulgar illustrators – probably from the Lower School – and not by Wodehouse himself.) Our envy – when we were schoolboys –

was chiefly centred on the illusion that at the college they could get away with more 'ragging' and more extravagance of a gentlemanly kind than we ourselves could. Mr Green has a delightful account of the prospects before our betters in Wodehouse's day. Both father and son were destined for Hong Kong:

> By 1867 imperial traffic was brisk, as the British wandered the surface of the planet in search of either divine missions or increased dividends, or, better still if it could be arranged, both at the same time. Off they sailed down the sea lanes ... the brevet colonels flushed with the proud apoplexy of a recent mention in dispatches; horse-faced subalterns whose toothy sibilance would soon be whistling across the promontories of the North-west Frontier; staff majors grimly pursuing the carrot of a KCIE; ruddy adjutants whose leaden gallantries might before long be rattling the teacups of some half-forgotten hill station; reverend gentlemen dedicated to the export of their religion to areas which had known their own when the English were still daubing their rumps with berry juice ... all these men resolved to reconciling somehow the opposing ideals of playing the game and pinching someone else's property, and miraculously succeeding, at least in part.

Public schools with their devotion to sport and their insistence on a solid grounding in Greek and Latin and even modern languages – Mr Green mentions the effect of this excellent education on Raymond Chandler, who was at Dulwich after Wodehouse. (Chandler remarked that a classical education saves you from being fooled by pretentiousness.) The creator of Wooster was a star athlete and boxer and editor of the school mag to whom the composition of crisp rhymed couplets in Latin and Greek was second nature. Characteristically the eupeptic Wodehouse thought the college was bliss, boyhood was bliss, the suburb of Dulwich heaven, and he scorned people who said life at English Public Schools was hell. There were only two flaws. His father lost his money, and he was forced to chuck Oxford or Cambridge and to go and earn his living in a Lombard Street bank, from which he was sacked early on for an outrageous act in the tradition of Dulwich 'ragging': he defaced and tore out the first page of that sacred object in banking life, a new ledger.

[158]

Clearly, like his insuppressible Psmith, he had been taught nerve.

The other flaw – if it was really a flaw, for, a eupeptic by nature, he scarcely mentioned it – was that like so many of the imperial sons he was sent home from abroad to be boarded out at holiday institutions or other families and especially with aunts. One thinks of the long list of English writers to whom this occurred: Kipling, Maugham, Saki, Orwell, wounded men all who scarcely knew their mothers. Did Wodehouse settle for a paradise of childlike laughter because of this deprivation? Does his general ferocity about aunts – except the one called romping Aunt Dahlia – come from this? Perhaps so.

On the other hand many of those half-abandoned boys were not as afflicted as some critics think they ought logically to have been. The only faint distress Wodehouse records is boredom with his elders, which is surely a normal affliction. The only places he liked, after Dulwich, were places like rural Shropshire, Lord Emsworth's moss-eaten paradise. One thing about the eternal schoolboy is his exceptional spryness in plotting his own cheeky and ingenious way, doing what he liked at once, which was to scribble and earn his living. He got off the ground in early school stories. Mr Green says:

> By a freakish collusion between temperament and experience, those schooldays left Wodehouse with a commitment to the schoolboy sensibility to which he remained forever steadfast, and which had the unexpected effect of making his work unique. For although Psmith insisted on breaking out, he took with him the intellectual and emotional luggage of a schoolboy. He and his followers may have been at large in the world of great affairs, but they arrived there still acting and reacting like the fifth-formers they would always remain. That is why there can be no sex in Wodehouse's world, only romance, no morality, only posture, no dogma, only laughter ... only Wodehouse [among scores of writers] pursued the odd idea of disguising his fifth-formers as responsible citizens and letting them loose among grown men and women.

And he quotes J. B. Priestley's admiring judgement about Wodehouse's lifelong character:

. . . there is no sign of a mature man here. Together with his talent for the absurd, this explains his success.

The Drones Club was a schoolboy's ideal. So is every pretty, sly, sexless girl who knows how to make circles round any romantic fool – provided she does not wear glasses and has not been to the London School of Economics or Cambridge and has not read Freud. From housemaid to debutante – she has to retain the *savoir-faire* and the legs of the chorus.

The prestige of the school story – in which Wodehouse began his career – seems to be a special curiosity of English life, for generations. I rather think the taste has now gone, but it harks back to Victorian traditions of character building: *Tom Brown's Schooldays* and most obviously Frederic Farrar's book *Eric, or Little by Little*. When Wodehouse tore that page out of the sacred ledger at the London bank he tore up the old school tradition. Mr Green detects a moralistic opponent in Wodehouse's work: the famous but distinctly down-market stories of the *Magnet* and *Gem* examined by George Orwell and written for us lads of the Lower School who would never be more than pseudo gentlemen or 'cads'. But when Wodehouse left the bank to write popular sketches and quips for the newspapers and then went off to New York, on a boyish impulse, nominally because he wanted to meet a few American boxers, he in fact turned his skills to writing lyrics for the new kind of musical comedy.

Mr Green is an authority on this arcane aspect of his hero's life, which is little known to fans of his subsequent novels. On reflection, one sees that a classical scholar would have his sort of skill in playing with language of all kinds, and knowing how to make the lines short but true, light humour being one of the graces of a good education of the classical kind. But when he broke into the impertinent joy and invention in *Carry On, Jeeves*, he found himself as a writer. The pompous Sir Roderick is seen 'wolfing' a plateful of chicken fricassee and 'handing up his dinner-pail for a second instalment'; the awful Honoraria Glossop, who has the voice of 'a lion tamer', appals Wooster because she looks like what the law calls an 'Act of God. You might just as well blame a fellow for being run over

[160]

by a truck.' A professor has an eye 'like a haddock' and his wife the look of a woman who 'had had bad news round about the year 1900 and never really got over it'. (The phrase 'round about' has that sense of a great leap into timeless space which is present in all his fantasies.) Wooster worships his brainlessness as he worships his ties and is given to prosaically knowing *obiter dicta* passages that end in grotesque explosions of precision:

> It is a peculiar thing in life that the people you most particularly want to edge away from always seem to cluster round like a poultice.

When he meets a girl at a station in *Leave It to Psmith*, Wooster's clichés are lyrical:

> ... you are as fresh and blooming as – if I may coin a simile – a rose. How do you do it? When I arrived I was deep in alluvial deposits, and have only just managed to scrape them off.

Comic writing, at its best, is an inverted poetry. As for blasts of introspection, does anything equal Lord Emsworth's discovery that the one thing his ancient family had somehow lacked was 'a family curse', but now, thank God, he has got one: his son.

Mr Green quotes Frank Swinnerton as saying that Wodehouse's great gift in language and invention is 'an irresistible air of improvisation' which has the paradoxical effect of putting dash into the sly sententiousness of Edwardian prose. In sheer pace he outdoes his contemporaries. It is in this and his stirring-up of fantasy, as A. J. P. Taylor rightly says, that Wodehouse ranks with Firbank and Congreve. One of the tests of such a remark is to see Wodehouse slowed down on television. This is a visual and oral disaster. His people were not meant to be seen or even heard, but have to be inducted from the ridiculous page; and anyway his people completely fox the modern actor or actress, who overdress the accents.

Mr Green goes carefully into the row about the notorious broadcasts to his American friends from Germany when he was taken prisoner in France. The talks were harmless, innocent, and Wodehouse has long ago been forgiven even by the official classes and the law. He was as foolish in this episode as any of his grown-up schoolboys. He suffered and saw what an ass he had been. It is to the great credit of Malcolm Muggeridge that he came intelligently to Wodehouse's defence; but in Orwell's defence of Wodehouse Mr Green acutely sees that Orwell errs when he says that Wodehouse had an upper-class blindness to the threat of Nazism. Long before, in one of his stories, Wodehouse had made a savagely hilarious attack on dictators. Benign as he was, Wodehouse got his own back on enemies like the one-time ambassador in Paris and on A. A. Milne.

It does strike one that his time in the German prison camp unseated Wodehouse's judgement: also that in his long years in the United States he lost something of his native ground – as indeed the great Henry James may be thought to have done in Britain and Europe. Yet, when we think of Wodehouse's long and flourishing years in the United States, it strikes us that his fantastic England depended on his being distant from it, and even if not copied the American vernacular does loosen the waistcoat. His England, his romantic fools and villains, depend for their lives on being absurdities. If this is so, why do the British, who devoured and still devour his books, recognise themselves? I heard Auberon Waugh say the other afternoon that perhaps in their poetic moments the British secretly idle in the dream of being Psmiths, Woosters and Jeeveses and Emsworths in disguise. The never-never-land is irresistible. It abounds also in Dickens. Even the pose of making fun of ourselves may disguise a private ideal. All nationals seem to have another self, preoccupied with sustaining illusions. Isn't this what comedy is about?

Mary Wollstonecraft

THE STRENGTH OF AN INJURED SPIRIT

Biographies of Mary Wollstonecraft have usually dwelt, quite properly, on the historical influences that favoured her leap from a statement of the Rights of Man to her book *A Vindication of the Rights of Woman*, first published in 1792. Her new biographer, Eleanor Flexner, looks rather to those things in her upbringing and private character that turned a neurasthenic into a pioneer of feminism. The driving force, as in other outstanding founders, sprang from a sense of personal injustice and family torment; her vision was intimately connected with the wrongs of childhood.

If she is a sad figure she grasped the luck that was going in the century of her birth. The rise of Puritan individualism worked for and against women but it did create a new concern for education as the eighteenth century invented its modernising revolutions. The class conflict between the new middles and the aristocracy put vehemence into controversy. Piety swept forward into scorn. More important, this was the time when the woman reader and the woman writer appeared, either as the author or reader of trashy novels, religious tracts, and copybook guides or, more preciously, as the blue stocking. What a weapon intellectual snobbery is!

Even if the writers did nothing for female emancipation, they were *paid* for their work and, in this sense, emancipated themselves. Indeed women authors owe it to the eighteenth century that they have been liberated for pretty well 200 years in the profession and are in many respects better placed than men. Mary Wollstonecraft began her life as many poor, unmarried women did, by governessing and teaching, but she was able to migrate to literature with relative ease. Her school handbooks did well and the famous 'bible' – *A Vindication of the Rights of Woman* – ran to several editions. Godwin, the philosopher, whom she eventually married, had been forced to become a sponge on aristocratic Shelley.

In her first book, *Thoughts on the Education of Daughters*, published in 1786, she aimed 'to teach women to think' and 'to prepare a woman to fulfill the duties of a wife and mother . . . No employment of the mind is a sufficient excuse for neglecting domestic duties, and I cannot conceive that they are incompatible.' If she is remote from us, she put her finger on the central issue of her time. A marked boredom and often a disgust with domesticity are noticeable in the English novelists of the eighteenth century. Marriage is so often seen as a stagnant and even squalid condition for both sexes. Who, outside the Widow Wadman, would have cared to marry into the Shandy family and share its ill-managed torpor? And although Mary Wollstonecraft would not have agreed, the gallantry and frivolity of the upper classes which she denounced were also in a sense, a protest. Better to sin than to suckle until the state of medicine improved.

The eighteenth century was the classic period of the standing army; one of the witty passages of the *Vindication* contains a comparison of married women with soldiers:

> Standing armies can never consist of resolute, robust men; they may be welldisciplined machines, but they will seldom contain men under the influence of strong passions, or with very vigorous faculties. And as for any depth of understanding I will venture to affirm, that it is as rarely to be found in the army as amongst women; and the cause, I maintain, is the same. It may be further observed, that officers are also particularly attentive to their persons, fond of dancing, crowded rooms, adventure and ridicule . . . They were taught to please.

The consequence (says our educator) is that they acquire manners before morals and a knowledge of life before they have reflected on it.

> Satisfied with common nature, they become a prey to prejudices, and taking all their opinions on credit, they blindly submit to authority.

Men who are slaves to their mistresses tyrannise over their sisters, wives and daughters. The famous jeer that women cannot resist a uniform is refuted by Mary Wollstonecraft: 'Has not education placed them more on a level with soldiers than any other class of men?'

The *Vindication* is a passionate, assertive, headlong, slapdash book, terribly repetitious and exclamatory. The author flings herself whole upon the reader; anger is mixed with a piety that hardly conceals a long, personal pain. It is a book written out of unhappiness and frustration. The merit of Miss Flexner's study is that it examines a vigorous if unstable character with sympathy and patience.

Mary Wollstonecraft came from the rising middle class. The rise was effected by her grandfather, an ambitious weaver who, having established himself as the landlord of useful London properties, devoted the rest of his life to the ruling fantasy of his class: setting up as a country gentleman with a small estate. He wished to be like his betters. His son, Mary's father, inherited the fantasy but not the acumen; weaving went downhill, and after failing in the townee's dream of farming he became a careless speculator and a violent, spendthrift drunk who could not keep his hands off his children's money. Mary's childhood was wrecked by the scenes of violence between her father and her Irish mother, a woman beaten down who nevertheless obviously had some power of moral survival. The effect of the family drama was to arrest the emotional development of a girl who was well above the norm in intelligence. She made a stand for independence. She was a second child, a beauty of the heavy kind, not the favourite, but the most capable. She had a defiant self-knowledge and in a letter written when she was sixteen to a friend she says unpleasingly:

> I am a little singular in my thought of love and friendship. I must have first place or none.

This was ominous. She was already, says Miss Flexner,

> possessive, and highly sensitive. The slightest affront, often fancied rather than real, caused intense feelings of rejection and anger . . . she wrote bitter letters raking up past grievances.

But as the family went to pieces it was she who energetically took command of her sisters and emerged as strong and masterful. The effort of will, as with many domineering people, had its price in sudden losses of confidence and in lonely pathos. Her passionate friendships with one or two girls of her own age were part of a search for an alternative family, but they were dangerously demanding. The pattern remained in her relations with men later on in her life; she asked too much, either out of blinding innocence or the ineptitude that sometimes affects the brilliant. Miss Flexner says:

> Modern psychiatry has identified some of the symptoms of which Mary constantly complained – lassitude, depression, acute headaches and digestive difficulties – as symptoms of deeply repressed anger. She had ample reasons for it – at a society that thwarted women; at a father who had thrown away a comfortable endowment and mistreated both wife and children; and at a mother with inadequate understanding.

Another symptom of this formless anger was anxiety, 'the sense of I know not what'. It was to explode at a crisis in her thirties in a thorough attempt at suicide after she had been abandoned by one of the father figures – this time only too like her father – to whom such a temperament would be drawn.

The fatality of such a temperament in a woman of intelligence and charm is sad. Her high-mindedness was apt to be ruthless and her naïveté hard to credit. When she saw her sister miserable after a forced marriage and the birth of a child, she obliged the not very bright girl to leave her husband, leaving the baby behind! It is not surprising that the 'rescued' sister was embittered for the rest of her life. One must admire the vitality of the bossy girl who took over her family, but one is struck by her lack of knowledge of the heart. When in a gush of juvenile feeling she herself adopted a little girl she quickly grew tired of the responsibility. And, of course, having made her sisters dependent on her help in their school teaching, she aroused their sneers and jealousies when at last she gave up her schooling and governessing and courageously turned to her ambitions as a writer. They thought she had grown too big for her boots.

Her story, of course, makes clear the exasperating burden of petty domestic trials upon an independent intelligence. It is the old tale – brothers could get away, for better or worse, and were not much help. Mary Wollstonecraft's salvation and her belated growth into adulthood began when her publisher, Joseph Johnson, took paternal charge of her. A man of extraordinary benevolence, he took her in for a time and gave her literary work – a good deal of it translation. He saw the born journalist who needed the education of his clever, radical circle. Blake, Fuseli, Tom Paine and eventually Godwin belonged to it. She threw over the governessing and, intoxicated by good talk, her mind came to life.

True, she was reckless in judgement, not to say unscrupulous – she accused Burke of being bought by a government pension – but she succeeded to the point of notoriety. At thirty she was emotionally a schoolgirl liable to crushes; she developed a passion for Fuseli, and when one considers her Puritan hatred of sex and of her father's rage it is strange that she seems not to have been put out by Fuseli's temper and the blatant sexual imagery of his work. He was, of course, expert in disengaging the unconscious. His brilliant talk carried her away. She seems to have been unaware of her repressed sexuality. She pestered Fuseli as George Eliot – if she was indeed innocent – pestered Chapman, with a swamping superego. Still, it may not have been quite like that: Fuseli was happily married and Mary was showing a girlish hunger to belong to a family. She had the simplicity to propose to Mrs Fuseli that she should come and live with them. Mrs Fuseli discerned the egotist and showed her the door.

As Miss Flexner says, the friendship with Fuseli seems not only to have aroused her intellect but to have awakened her to the emotions that lay behind her earnest daydreaming. What followed was an emotional disaster. The French Revolution was in its idealistic phase and many English radicals rushed to Paris. Her reputation as an educationalist was well known but surely she went rather far in offering to advise the French authorities on the education of French women! The Terror stopped that. She was horrified and frightened. As an Englishwoman she was in danger of arrest. She turned to an American speculator and plotting political agent, Gilbert Imlay, a liaison began, and he saved her by saying she was his wife.

Imlay was in fact a charming rascal. He was a fugitive from justice in Kentucky and one can see that an inexperienced, intellectual woman of her kind was likely to fall for the dubious gallantry she had always attacked. Imlay was not one to stay long with any woman; he was always disappearing. Mary was soon pregnant and his absences grew longer. He tricked her into going on a mission for him in Scandinavia – a quarter of

Copenhagen had been destroyed by fire when she got there – and on her return she found him living with another woman in London.

It was now that the basic rage of her nature (the inheritance, no doubt, of her father's rage) burst out in a very determined attempt at suicide by drowning. She planned it thoroughly, even going to the length of letting the rain soak her clothes so that she would sink at once. Fortunately she was rescued. It was Godwin's friendship that saved her mind. When she was thirty-seven she married him and then, once more, she was a victim. Her death in childbirth is the final injustice. Her daughter by Godwin grew up to be Mary Shelley, who, tormented in her turn, revered her mother's work but refused to have anything to do with female emancipation. The idea faded until Mill's essay on the *Subjection of Women* – a far better book than the *Vindication* – vigorously revived it for the mid-Victorians.

Miss Flexner has gone carefully into Mary Wollstonecraft's writings and, as she says, her distinction is that her opinions came from her experience of ordinary people she knew. But when she turned to novel writing she could not make such people live. Earnest, bold, a teacher to the backbone, she was really self-absorbed, too little resilient to allow other people to exist except as generalities or projections of her opinions. Her tale is painful but she made a great deal of an injured spirit. The tragedy is that under Godwin's influence her powers might have grown; he certainly conquered her touchiness after a patient struggle.

LIST OF BOOKS

SHOLOM ALEICHEM
The Best of Sholom Aleichem, ed. Irving Howe and Ruth R. Wisse (Simon & Schuster, 1980).

ISAAC BABEL
The Lonely Years 1925–1939 by Isaac Babel, ed. Nathalie Babel and trans. Andrew R. MacAndrew and Max Hayward (Farrar, Straus, 1964).
You Must Know Everything: Stories 1915–1937 by Isaac Babel, ed. Nathalie Babel and trans. Max Hayward (Farrar, Straus, 1969).
The Collected Stories by Isaac Babel, trans. Walter Morison and introduced by Lionel Trilling (Methuen, 1957; Penguin Books, Harmondsworth, 1961).

SIMONE DE BEAUVOIR
Old Age by Simone de Beauvoir, trans. Patrick O'Brian (André Deutsch and Weidenfeld & Nicolson, 1972).

GERALD BRENAN
Thoughts in a Dry Season: A Miscellany by Gerald Brenan (Cambridge University Press, 1978).

ROBERT BROWNING
The Book, the Ring, and the Poet: A Biography of Robert Browning by William Irvine and Park Honan (The Bodley Head, 1975).

BRUCE CHATWIN
On the Black Hill by Bruce Chatwin (Penguin Books, 1984).

FLAUBERT AND TURGENEV
Flaubert and Turgenev: A Friendship in Letters. The Complete Correspondence, ed. and trans. by Barbara Beaumont (Norton, 1985).

HUMBOLDT
Humboldt and the Cosmos by Douglas Botting (Michael Joseph, 1973).

MOLLY KEANE
Good Behaviour by Molly Keane (Knopf, 1981).
Time After Time by Molly Keane (Knopf, 1984).

[169]

LE ROY LADURIE
Montaillou: The Promised Land of Error by Emmanuel Le Roy Ladurie, trans. Barbara Bray (Vintage Books, 1979).

LORCA
The Assassination of Federico García Lorca by Ian Gibson (Penguin Books, 1983).

ANDRÉ MALRAUX
Picasso's Mask by André Malraux, trans. and annotated by June Guicharnaud with Jacques Guicharnaud (Henry Holt, 1976).

THOMAS MANN
Thomas Mann: The Making of an Artist 1875–1911 by Richard Winston (Knopf, 1981).

V. S. NAIPAUL
Among the Believers: An Islamic Journey by V. S. Naipaul (Knopf, 1981).

GEORGE ORWELL
The Crystal Spirit: A Study of George Orwell by George Woodcock (Schocken Books, 1984).

JOHN OSBORNE
A Better Class of Person: An Autobiography 1929–1956 by John Osborne (Faber & Faber, 1985).

WALKER PERCY
Love in the Ruins by Walker Percy (Farrar, Straus, 1971).
The Moviegoer by Walker Percy (Knopf, 1961).

FORREST REID
The Green Avenue: The Life and Writings of Forrest Reid 1875–1947 by Brian Taylor (Cambridge University Press, 1980).

SALMAN RUSHDIE
Midnight's Children by Salman Rushdie (Knopf, 1980).

ANTOINE DE SAINT-EXUPÉRY
Saint-Exupéry: A Biography by Marcel Migeo, trans. Herma Griffault and McGraw-Hill Book Company Inc. (Macdonald, 1961).

BRUNO SCHULZ
The Street of Crocodiles by Bruno Schulz, trans. Celina Wieniewska and introd. Jerzy Ficowski (Penguin Books, 1977).

BERNARD SHAW
Collected Letters Vol. 1, 1874–1897 ed. Dan H. Laurence (Dodd, Mead, 1965).

JOHN UPDIKE
Rabbit Is Rich by John Updike (Knopf, 1981).

REBECCA WEST
Rebecca West: A Life by Victoria Glendinning (Knopf, 1987).

OSCAR WILDE
Oscar Wilde by Richard Ellmann (Knopf, 1988).

P. G. WODEHOUSE
P. G. Wodehouse: A Literary Biography by Benny Green (Pavilion Books in association with Michael Joseph, 1981).

MARY WOLLSTONECRAFT
Thoughts on the Education of Daughters by Mary Wollstonecraft (London, 1786).
A Vindication of the Rights of Woman by Mary Wollstonecraft (London, 1792; Penguin Classics 1988).
Mary Wollstonecraft A Biography by Eleanor Flexner (Coward, McCann & Geoghegan, 1972).

V. S. PRITCHETT was born in England in 1900. One of the great men of twentieth-century literature, Sir Victor is recognized as a formidable critic, novelist, writer of short stories, travel writer, autobiographer, and biographer. He was knighted in 1975 and is a foreign honorary member of the American Academy of Arts and Letters and of the Academy of Arts and Sciences. He lives in London with his wife, Dorothy.